SIGNY FOREVER

A WOLF SHIFTER FATED MATES REVERSE HAREM ROMANCE

BILLIONAIRE WOLVES SERIES
BOOK SEVEN

CHARMAINE LOUISE SHELTON

CONTENTS

WANT FREE BOOKS?

Want to know what happened to Jagger's best friend Dylan? Find out in *Dylan The Rogue: A Wolf Shifter Fated Mates Paranormal Romance* **your FREE Book!**

Click Cover Below or visit **bit.ly/ CLBooksDylanTheRogue** to subscribe to my newsletter for latest news and launches, books from my author friends, and sizzling reads in book promotions. Plus, start reading the steamy fated mates romance for bad boy wolf shifter Dylan.

To read her current works, visit her Ream Stories account bit.ly/CharmaineLouiseBooksCoterie.

ABOUT SIGNY FOREVER: A WOLF SHIFTER FATED MATES REVERSE HAREM ROMANCE

My wolf shifter fated mates claimed me. But will we make it to our happily ever after, and will it last forever?

Garrett the grumpy leader whose glacial eyes pierce my soul.

Dolph the comforting beta whose musky masculine scent makes me shiver.

Colin the brute enforcer whose snark is as good as his bite.

I'm their fated mate and their Queen of the New York Wolves Pack.

*Their spicy reverse harem paranormal romance is part three of the standalone trilogy in the sizzling **Billionaire Wolves***

Series of interconnecting stories featuring wolf shifter fated mates romance. Get a glimpse of their dynamism in other books.

Anthem: "Again" Lenny Kravitz

https://www.youtube.com/watch?v=eW2qlKa6oHw

Visit CharmaineLouiseBooks.com

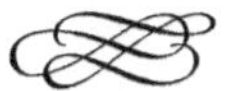

CHAPTER 1

Signy

THEY LIED TO ME.

Nothing in this world could prepare me for their betrayal. For the subsequent pain. It ravages my heart. Each chamber shreds as their three threads spasm. They wobble, raising bile to the back of my throat. My body hunches as I swallow the acid with a whimper knowing what the spasms mean.

Our connections as fated mates—an invisible super-highway—relay our emotions to the others. Carried over a distance to a degree, even when we're apart.

But this agony? So sharp—as precise as a heart surgeon's scalpel? It can mean one thing only. Garrett,

Dolph, and Colin have severe injuries. Or, the gods forbid, worse.

"No! No! No!"

My screams reverberate around our bedroom. I sit up in the massive new bed we share. My stacked palms press against my chest, directly over my bleeding heart. I shake my head as I rail on until sobs choke me. My throat sore, too thick to swallow. Lungs burn from lack of oxygen. Head pounds. Eyes squeeze shut, I collapse against the pillows, still clutching my throbbing chest.

"Please no," I whisper hoarsely. "Garrett... Dolph... Colin... please be alive. Come back to me. *You promised.* Don't let it be a lie, like your promise we'd be together always. And you left me here."

Another soul-stealing sob racks my body.

Only months ago, they found me amongst the wreckage of my private jet after it crashed during a freak blizzard. Seriously wounded and placed in a medically induced coma, I awoke with no memory of who I was or even that I was a wolf shifter. I refused to believe their words. Impossible. Until they shifted into three massive wolves.

Even more shocking was beta Dolph's claim I was their fated mate. A rare pairing between wolf shifters planned by the gods. Alpha Garrett felt the connection too. But he was reluctant to act on it given the enemies they face on dangerous missions and his unwavering vow to not put me in harm's way. Enforcer Colin outright refused to interact with me beyond snarky, hurtful comments.

But the forced proximity of being stranded inside The

Fortress—the New York Wolves Pack's enforcer training facility—during the unceasing blizzard changed the dynamic amongst us. Dolph provided the comfort I needed as I struggled with who I was and what my future may hold. Garrett's power as Alpha drew me to him despite the barrier he erected to protect me. The strength Colin exuded as the fearless bad boy who taunted me made me face the situation and work to overcome the fear amnesia caused.

And then the carnal moments within the fortified walls of The Fortress. Kisses and touches. Pinnacles of ecstasy. Garrett and Dolph pleasured me, while Colin's aloofness heightened the sexual tension thrumming between us. Even though they didn't convince me of being a she-wolf or their fated mate, I couldn't deny my attraction to them.

But monsters kidnapped me. Planned to breed me for pups they'd sell on the underground market. A highly profitable enterprise at the expense of the she-wolves and human females forcibly turned into shifters they capture. For decades, run by a syndicate of rings led by deviant male wolf shifters.

Unlike some females who they trapped for years, I was fortunate my mates rescued me within days. And even better—Estrid, the she-wolf who cared for me—was Colin's mother, who he thought abandoned him as a pup. Which explains his distrust of mates, fated or otherwise. The rescue turned into a reunion for mother and son.

However, the elation didn't last long. My mind was in turmoil from recovering my memory thanks to a blow to my head from Blaise—the alpha of that ring. Fear drove me back to Moon Island, the home of my Miami Wolves Pack. My older brothers Jagger—the Alpha—and Viggo Larson were more than happy to bring me back to our family and our pack despite, or because of, me being the fated mate to three males.

Only for me to realize I needed them, couldn't live without them. And the feeling was mutual, as they proved when they arrived uninvited on Moon Island at risk of a brutal fight with my pack. They faced off with my brothers along with Tag Dahl, Rust Ingolf, and Dylan Vang—their best friends and, by default, more older brothers. But as they say, love conquers all. I flew back to Moen Island—the New York Wolves Pack home off the coast of East Hampton, Long Island.

They completed our bond by issuing their claiming bites on my neck to embed serum laced with their scent beneath my skin, marking me as theirs forever and as their Queen.

Or so I thought.

That was a week ago. Now, they've gone to battle more monsters and to save more females and pups from an auction. A dangerous mission with members from the six packs—New York, Miami, Aspen, Las Vegas, Sedona, Los Angeles—converging on the location.

The threads of our mate bond relay their torment. My mates' lives are in question. Our future unknown.

I grab fistfuls of my ebony black hair and tug as I keen.

"Gods! Why would you bring us together only to tear us apart?"

Nothing but my labored breathing answers me as it fills an empty bedroom redecorated for four. I tug until silky strands slip from my fingers, collecting on the tangled sheets around me.

The ring of my mobile startles me.

My eyes pop open. Tears drip down my face. I scramble from the center of the bed in a nest of their t-shirts cloaked in their comforting scents. My hand shakes as I reach for my mobile on the nightstand.

Please be them!

Thyra Moen's name appears on the screen. *Damn!*

A call from Garrett's younger sister and the pack's tech wiz? Now? She must know something.

Gods, please!

I accept the call with one hand and press the other against my chest to slow my racing heart.

"What happened?" I croak, tears dripping onto the mobile screen.

Whimpering travels over the line.

My eyes close as I sink into the mattress heavily. My teeth dig into my bottom lip to bite back the wail that threatens to pour from my mouth.

If Thyra, who's tough and takes no shit from anyone, not even from her Alpha brother, is crying, the situation is far worse than I imagine. And she provided the details of their mission. One I begged them not to take.

But how could they not?

They're not just billionaires who run Moen, Inc.—a multibillion-dollar arms and aircraft manufacturing company. They're Green Berets devoted to eliminating the breeding rings. A vow they cannot renege. Even after claiming their mate and leaving me to deal with the aftermath without them.

I take a deep, cleansing breath and beg the gods for positive news from Thyra, despite her whimpers.

"What happened?" I repeat.

Thyra expels a long breath. A beat later, she responds.

"Something went terribly wrong... I—I lost contact with them... all of them... Trackers for Garrett, Dolph, and Colin show their vitals... their vitals are... weak..." she stutters, the last words whispered.

A knot forms in my chest. My heart skips a beat as lungs constrict. My breath skips. Stars dance behind my closed eyelids. The mobile crunches under my white-knuckled grip.

"What does that mean, Thyra?"

I refuse to believe my mates left this world. We've only just begun to live our life together. Accepted being destined for each other. Completed our bond. Planned to have our mate bonding ceremony before all packs. We haven't had time to discuss pups of our own. So much left to do and to share. My heart and my womb clench.

No! Thyra must be mistaken. My mind replays her words.

I lost contact with them... all of them.

The breath escapes my lungs in a gut-wrenching howl.

Jagger, Tag, and Dylan, along with Miami Wolves Pack enforcers, joined the mission too. Garrett placed the call to all packs. Each responded with their Alphas and their enforcers to battle as one to destroy the ring, as our history and connections require in times of need.

Several millennia ago, Scandinavian Viking wolf shifters sailed from the Old World and landed along the East Coast of what's now the United States. The six packs headed by best friends who sought new lands moved throughout the continent to form territories, with ours settling here. We maintain close ties with our brethren through friendship, mating, and business. Plus, our Ruling Council gatherings keep us informed of happenings throughout the packs.

This mission impacts every single one of the six packs.

But for me, it's especially devastating. My mates *and* my family? Inconceivable.

Do Sage, Wren, and Sasha sense a change in their bonds with Jagger, Tag, and Dylan? I must call them after Thyra.

"The change in vitals shows injuries. The trackers don't offer specifics. But monitors the levels, and theirs are extremely low…"

Thyra's voice catches as she sobs.

"This is my fault! I sent them out there! I should have checked the intel from the Dark Web more thoroughly. What an amateur move… *Oh, gods!* What have I done?"

She wails uncontrollably. More words of guilt fill in the spaces between her cries.

Even as I want to blame her for telling them about the

chatter she read online, I can't. My heart breaks anew at her pain. This is not her fault. The instinct to comfort her pushes my agony aside.

"Thyra, stop," I say, then repeat it when she continues berating herself.

She pauses, and I continue, "You had no way to know what they would face once they arrived at the location. You could only share the messages you found and provide the coordinates. Do not blame yourself. Okay?"

She hiccups before she responds, "I guess."

It's critical for her to focus. Regardless of her current beliefs, she is the tech wiz. We need her to figure out what the hell happened and the current state of the location. Get back in front of her four monitors and type away on her keyboard.

I take another deep, cleansing breath to center myself before I ask her to return to her computer. It's probably the last thing she wants to do. But she must. All of us must push through, including me—the pack Luna. Albeit the newly made pack Luna with zero experience. *Gah!*

Shaking my head, I ignore the flutter of butterflies in my belly and press on hoping to infuse strength in myself even as I attempt to so in Thyra. Another breath, and I speak.

"Good. We need you to set aside those thoughts and figure out what happened. Okay?"

She hesitates, then agrees.

"Thank you. Now, I have to call my sister-in-law Luna Sage. I'll come to your office when I'm done."

Thyra and I end our call.

I run my fingers through my tangled hair as I consider the possibility my brothers are fine. But only Sage, Wren, and Sasha can provide that answer. My eyes close. I pray to the gods for the strength to handle whatever they tell me about their connections to my brothers.

With dread weighing on my heart, I tap Sage's name in the contacts app on my mobile.

CHAPTER 2

Signy

"I KNOW."

Sage answers the FaceTime on the first ring. Her calm voice contrasts with my blubbering upon awakening to my worse nightmare. Flushed toffee cheeks and red-rimmed emerald green eyes are the only signs of her distress. She blinks and swipes an errant tear clinging to the tips of her long eyelashes. After her throat works around a swallow, she continues.

"I awoke to explosions and intense pain through my mate bond with Jagger. Wren and Sasha experienced the same. They're on their way to my house now."

"My parents? Have you spoken to them? They're next on my list."

Sage nods.

"Sigrid's mother's instinct sensed a disturbance in her family. She called me immediately since Jagger is on the mission."

Sage's voice wavers as she dabs her cheek with trembling fingers. Her eyes glisten with tears. Clearing her voice, she continues.

"I—I told her about my vision through Jagger's eyes..."

My breath stalls.

Sage is a powerful immortal witch turned she-wolf with Jagger's claiming bite. She wields never-before-seen magick because of his DNA mixing with hers. As the High Witch of the Coven of the South and the head of the Witch Council, she governs all their kind.

Jagger and Sage's taboo love survived years of separation caused by her mother and my father. Since Jagger happened upon Sage, their love grows stronger. Along with her magick, their intense love strengthens their mate bond beyond emotions to sharing each other's sight.

I hate to imagine what she witnessed at the location and her helplessness. But I need to know what happened. To have confirmation of the extent of their injuries or if they're alive. A shudder runs through me at the thought of them screaming in agony or, the gods forbid, not moving at all.

Sage stares in the distance as she recalls Jagger's viewpoint. Although her voice remains steady, tears stream down her ashen cheeks. This time, she doesn't bother to wipe them away. They slip from her eyes unabated as she describes the grisly scene. Sitting unnaturally still, her disembodied voice drones on, providing gut-wrenching details, even as Wren and Sasha appear beside her on the mobile screen.

Their pale, tear-stained faces crease with sobs as they listen. Wren's mink brown eyes flick to mine at the mention of Garrett's name. I stare mutely at Sage as my mind attempts to process her words. My gaze swings to Sasha at her pitiful cry. A curtain of ash blonde hair sweeps across her wan alabaster face as she lowers her head. Her shoulders shake with her cries and Russian words of heartache. My heart clenches for all of us.

A knock at my bedroom door draws my attention. I carry my mobile with me as I rise from the bed, slip into a silk robe, and open the door. Arne and Idonea stand before me. Arne's eyebrows dip low as his eyes spark with anger. Idonea covers her mouth with a shaky hand as she hears Sage describing the scene.

I embrace her and gesture at the sofa in the sitting room. Arne spins on his heel and stalks past the sofa to pace before the windows. Idonea and I settle on the sofa and shift our gazes to the mobile screen.

As Sage continues, more figures appear behind those in her living room. My father, Marcus, holds my distraught mother against his side as they walk towards Sage. Viggo and Rust stand in intense conversation while Maya and Natalie—Rust's fated mate—wrap their arms around Wren and Sasha. Not wanting to disturb Sage as she speaks, they nod at me.

All our gazes shift behind them as eleven females appear out of thin air. Identical twins with manes of ebony hair and emerald green eyes, petite and curvy, walk amongst them. I recognize them as Sage's younger sisters, Willow and Lillie. The others I don't know. They offer comforting touches to the others as they move to Sage's side. They mouth hellos to Idonea and to me. She nods, closing her eyes while I incline my head.

Once Sage finishes, her gaze returns to the mobile. Emerald eyes flash with determination to replace their vacant expression.

"As witches—with me an exception as the Miami Wolves Pack's Luna—we do not interfere in wolf shifter affairs. However, now my mate's life is in peril. I dare anyone—witch or wolf shifter or the gods themselves—to stop me from going to him and from eliminating all threats to him and to the others."

Her eyes flash with her ebony wolf close to the surface as she glances around at us. She pins Marcus and Sigrid with a challenging stare. Although Sage has forgiven them for separating Jagger and her, it's clear she hasn't forgotten. My parents bow their heads and add their voices to the rest of us in agreement. Sage continues.

"My sisters, coven members, and I will use our teleportation magick to reach the location now. Together, we will secure the area and erect a protective barrier to enable us to work without interference."

"Luna, no disrespect. But Jagger will have our balls if we

let you go without us," Viggo says, as he waves his hand between Rust and himself.

Sage opens her mouth, then closes it and nods.

"Fine," she says. "And Maya and Natalie can thank me later for allowing you to remain intact."

The bit of levity eases the tension.

But I cannot smile. I want to go.

But before I speak, Sage turns her gaze to me.

"Signy, I know you're eager to reach your mates. But it's best if we handle the situation. We need to use all our focus to heal the damage inflicted on everyone. I will update you as able. I hope you understand."

Tears well in my eyes. But I whisper my acceptance. It's best to set aside my need to be with my mates and allow Sage and the others to work their magick unencumbered.

Idonea rubs my arm. My watery gaze moves to her.

"Don't worry. Let Sage do what needs to be done. You—as Luna—need to lead our pack in Garrett's absence. First, inform every one of the situation, then determine who will run Moen, Inc."

"Indeed, Signy. You have much to do," Arne adds as he stops pacing and faces me.

A cold sweat breaks out over my skin at the thought of leading the second-most powerful pack on my own. Granted, I grew up the daughter of an Alpha and Luna and am familiar with pack law and hierarchy. But being on the sidelines and not the quarterback is a whole other ballgame. And being new to this pack?

Will the members respect me?

Will they accept my leadership?

Will they turn to Idonea as the former Luna and disregard me? Her very name means suitable. More so than I am.

Worse yet, will they expect Arne to take over as he did when the blizzard trapped Garrett and made him unreachable at The Fortress?

On top of it all, my heart bleeds for my mates. My mind wants to focus on them, not on leading the New York Wolves Pack.

Gods help me!

Warm hands squeeze mine. They drag me from the inner turmoil. My eyes lift to Idonea's face.

Glacial blue eyes so like her son's shine with compassion as she stares into my ice blue eyes, reaching into the very depths of my soul. I sense she sees my despair. Her head nods as she tightens her grip on my hands, anchoring me to the present and away from my mind-numbing doubts.

"Signy, sweetheart, I can only imagine the pain you must feel and the concern you must have for not one but for three mates. But know this, I support you and will mentor you as best I can to lead our pack. You are our Luna now, and you must step into the role no matter the circumstances."

Her warmth rolls through me, sparking an ember deep within me. A bit of hope flares.

"I will offer my input," Arne starts, and I lift my gaze to the former Alpha. He nods and continues. "But not in front of the pack. They must see you as our leader, not as a figurehead for me in Garrett's absence."

His voice catches on the last few words. He clears his throat and blinks back the tears shining in his eyes. His sizable hands fist at his sides as he pivots and continues his pacing.

I watch Garrett's formidable father rein in his emotions as I struggle to do the same with mine. A tear slips from the corner of my eye. I swipe it and shake my head to clear the vestiges of doubt. The ember glows with determination.

"Thank you. Thank you, both," I say to my in-laws, then turn back to the mobile screen. My eyes focus on Sage's. "Would you like Thyra to provide you with satellite images to prepare you before you go?"

Sage shakes her head as she draws in a deep breath.

"I've seen enough. We must leave. Now."

I too inhale deeply and nod.

"Please contact me as soon as you can. May the gods be with you to bring our mates and as many others as possible home."

"We will," Sage rasps before she ends the FaceTime.

I stare at my mobile screen. The app icons blur as a pep talk runs through my head. Idonea and Arne give me the silence I need to fan the ember into a steady flame. It spreads until it licks at the doubt and singes it from my soul.

I must be strong for my mates, not allow fear to control me. They would want me to step up to my role as Luna and lead our pack, no matter the situation. I must set aside my feelings, at least until I return to the comfort of our bed, surrounded by their scents. Then I can let it all go. Cry until no further tears flow.

A final deep, cleansing breath girds me as I rise from the sofa. My gaze flicks between Idonea and Arne.

"I will change and call for the pack to meet at once."

CHAPTER 3

"WHAT DO YOU MEAN, 'EXPLOSIONS?'"

"My gods! So, it's true? I felt my mate's pain, but..."

"Are they all... gone?"

"What about Alpha Garrett?"

The walls of the pack meeting room vibrate with questions, screams, and growls.

Mournful howls slice through my heart, reopening the barely healed gashes. Unconsciously, my fingers grip the front of my sweater, pressing the heel of my hand against my fragile heart. My vision blurs with unshed tears. Instead of answers, a gasp escapes my parted lips.

"We have to get to them!"

A burly wolf I recognize as an enforcer shouts as he jumps to his feet. Others pick up his rallying cry. The room erupts into further chaos.

My alarmed gaze swings between Idonea and Arne, who flank me on the dais. He gives an imperceptible shake of his head while keeping his eyes on the group. Idonea locks eyes with mine. I sense her strength flowing to me. It stills my racing pulse long enough for me to refocus.

"Alpha Arne! What do we do?"

The call from another male for direction from someone other than me, the Luna, flames the fire within me. Now is the moment to exert my leadership, even if my pulse increases at his words.

I send a prayer to the gods to guide my words and actions before I address the restless group.

"As your Luna—"

"Alpha Arne, what do *you* say?"

The older male eyes me with disdain before he flicks his gaze from me to focus on Arne, who turns to me.

My cheeks heat as the male cuts me off with blatant disregard for my position in the pack. Regardless of how new to the New York Wolves I may be, I am the mate to the Alpha making me the Luna. Pack hierarchy calls for respect. And I will demand it.

I recall memories of my mother commanding enforcers to patrol the borders of our camp in the Everglades and addressing the Ruling Council while my father was traveling for Larson Enterprises, Inc. business. She was confident and accepted no opposition. Head held high, eyes sharp, and spine ramrod straight, she leads as Luna.

With a deep breath, I draw from those memories and the fierce look in Idonea's eyes. I emulate them as I raise my hand for silence and pin the male with an intense stare.

"What is your name?"

He blinks and meets my gaze.

I arch an eyebrow.

"Victor."

I cock my head.

Realization dawns in his brown eyes.

"Vi—Victor, Luna," he stammers under my scrutiny. His feet shift as I continue to stare at him until he lowers his eyes in respect. "My apologies, Luna."

Silence descends on the room as he sits. All await my next words. With a satisfied nod, I address him and the other members, who stare at me in wonder.

"Our pack and those of the other five have suffered tremendously. We will learn the full extent once Luna Sage contacts me."

Wanting to connect with the members, I pause and glance around at their faces. Many tearstained and eyes full of anguish or anger return my gaze. My heart clenches as I see my pain and my rage reflected at me. The urge to soothe them grows from the fire in my soul.

"It may seem impossible to fathom the losses we'll face. But know we will face them together as a pack. All will share your pain and anger. No one member is alone. We are one. As your Luna, I will lead the New York Wolves

Pack until my mate and our Alpha Garrett returns to us. I will do my absolute best for our pack."

The older male who challenged my authority rises from his chair. His brown eyes blaze with his inner wolf close to the surface. His fists clench at his sides.

My wolf rises from her haunches with a snarl, prepared to defend me when summoned.

"Luna, I stand with you and will do as you command. Should you call for a counterattack, I will be the first to step forward to avenge our pack."

Others call out their support until the room rings with their cries, stomping feet, and ferocious howls. The wave of energy swirls around to envelop our pack, uniting us as one.

My heart soars as I absorb the positivity despite the undercurrent of sadness. My wolf lifts her muzzle and joins in the wolf song.

"Well done, Luna."

Arne bows his head in deference.

"You're a natural Luna, Signy. Trust in your instinct," Idonea adds.

"Thank you," I murmur, then send a silent prayer to the gods for instilling the strength I need to lead my pack.

The next few hours fly by. I direct the remaining enforcers to prep for a counterattack with the latest info from Thyra. Then I speak with the pack doctor to ensure the hospital is ready for the return of the wounded. Next, I meet with the elders, including Arne and Idonea, to plan for the less fortunate. The last task is to decide who will run Moen, Inc. in the interim.

After the elders leave the room, I turn to Arne.

"My understanding is Randel handled the affairs of Moen, Inc. while the blizzard stranded Garrett, Dolph, and Colin at The Fortress."

My mates run the company with Garrett as the CEO, Dolph the COO, and Colin the Chief Counsel. If they entrust Garrett's younger brother in their absence, I do, too. He can keep me abreast of the happenings and with Arne, we can make decisions. For now. Since in my heart, I know my mates will return to me and will resume their places.

"Yes, Randel is the CFO. He's fully immersed in the business and can handle the company until the others return," Arne responds, adding emphasis to the last part.

His adamancy my mates will return well enough to run the company bolsters my confidence. I smile and nod with a sigh.

"Take heart, Signy. It may not be as bad as we think. Enhanced healing helps our kind to withstand much more than a fragile human. Plus, they're young males in excellent condition. We must focus on the best scenario."

"Yes. Now. Let's get you home to eat. You must keep up your strength," Idonea adds with a motherly smile. "You'll be of little help to the pack if you don't take care of yourself."

As we enter the lobby of the building used for our pack meetings and for Moen, Inc. offices on the island,

Thyra, Randel, and his mate Vera, along with Dolph and Colin's parents, await us. Their mothers—Revna and Estrid—wrap me in an embrace as they murmur words of support.

"You did well, Signy," Birger, Dolph's father, says as Colin's father Brandt voices his agreement.

"Your mates would be proud of you," he adds.

My heart stutters as my hold on control falters. Words fail me. I nod and close my eyes to stop the flow of tears.

"Come, let's get you home. You need to eat and rest," Idonea says as she guides us towards the exit.

We travel in SUVs on the main road of Moen Island. Instead of appreciating the beauty of spring blossoming all around, my thoughts turn inward. I stare sightlessly out the window. Even the warmth of the sun cannot revive me. I yearn for my mates. Only they can bring joy back to my heart.

"Come, Signy. We're here."

Estrid's gentle voice reaches past my despair. She squeezes my forearm as her amber eyes—identical to Colin's—search my face. Another squeeze, and she slides from the seat, bringing me with her.

Just as she cared for me when Blaise held me captive, Estrid ushers me through the double doors of the mansion. Its emptiness sends an icy shiver down my spine. I shudder, and she squeezes my arm. Quickly, she settles me on the oversized leather sofa, where Thyra curls into one corner and stares at the hearth.

As Estrid drapes a cashmere blanket over my legs, she

says, "Wait a moment while Idonea, Revna, Vera, and I fix lunch for you. Then we'll leave you to rest."

As she rises, I clutch her arm, suddenly panicked.

"No, please stay… I don't want to be alone. Please."

"Of course, honey," she says as she pats my hand, then nods when I loosen my grip.

"I'll get a fire going," Brandt says.

"And I'll get something to heat us up from the inside," Arne adds as he strides to the liquor cabinet. I watch as he removes the stopper of a crystal decanter. Prisms dance across the wall. As he pours the rich mahogany liquid into matching tumblers, it glints in the light.

Randel carries three glasses and sits on the leather chair beside me. He offers a smile as he hands one to Thyra and another to me.

"Try not to worry, sis. Those three are resilient and survived unimaginable missions as Green Berets and those since they've retired from on-the-records service. The gods have not finished with them on this plane."

"I second that," Birger says as he raises his tumbler for a healthy swig.

"Hear, hear."

"Believe it."

As though sensing the conversation, the ring of my mobile pierces the air. The tumbler nearly falls from my hand as I shift on the sofa to retrieve the mobile from my jeans pocket. Deftly, Randel catches the glass and places it on the side table.

The air sparks with electricity as tension surrounds us.

My blood pressure skyrockets at the sight of Sage's name on the screen. My hand trembles as a finger jabs the accept button. I swallow to work around the sudden lump in my throat.

"Please," I croak in answer as the call connects on speaker.

"Jagger and the rest of the pack are here on Moon Island. My sisters and I will use our teleportation magick to leave here and return to the scene. From there, we'll bring your mates along with the others from your pack to you. Meet us at the hospital."

My mouth opens. But words fail to come forth. Instead, questions race through my mind.

Does she mean they're alive?

And if so, did the enhanced healing do it or her magick?

How are Jagger, Tag, and Dylan? The males? What happened with the she-wolves and human females turned into wolf shifters?

"Signy? I have to hurry. Did you hear me?"

A chorus of yeses jerk me back. I glance around to find everyone staring at me. Idonea takes my mobile.

"Thank you, Sage, for saving our sons and the others," she says in a tone laced with relief.

"Don't thank me yet. Much work needs to be done, and sadly, we couldn't help everyone—"

Urgent voices in the background interrupt her. Muffled conversation follows before she returns.

"I must go. Be ready."

As Sage ends the call, Idonea collapses onto the sofa

between Thyra and me. The cries of Revna and Estrid join hers. My hands fly to my face as a choked sob tears from my aching chest. My wolf's dejected howl reverberates in my head even as a grief-stricken cry pours from my mouth.

"Gods! Please!"

CHAPTER 4

arrett

"THE LAYOUT MATCHES the images provided by Thyra. It's their typical setup, with a building for the auction surrounded by trucks with the females and pups. The only differences are the additional vehicles, presumably from the bidders. We go in as planned. Kill all members of the ring but the leaders. Detain the bidders with the silver handcuffs and ankle shackles. We will transport them to the Aspen pack's lodge. Understood?"

As I voice my command over the earpieces worn by each wolf shifter from the six assembled packs, my eyes focus on Dolph and Colin. They return my determined gaze with their own. I imagine it's as hard for them to set aside the vision of Signy crying at the mansion as it is for me. But we must. This mission cannot fail.

The chatter Thyra deciphered off the Dark Web shows a new breeding ring cropped up after we took out Blaise and Bernard's—the largest one. This ring was second to theirs as the most active. Based on the outskirts of the Aspen Wolves' territory, it's close to our border with them. This new threat took over the contacts the other one established. The chatter revealed a big shipment with a subsequent auction.

That's bad enough. But to add to the wrongness, the ring targeted daughters and a sister of Alphas, the newly sought-after targets. They start the bids at $1 million each. Blaise upped the offerings of desirable she-wolves by capturing Signy—an Alpha's daughter and mated to an Alpha. The auction begins tonight.

The Alpha of the Aspen Wolves Pack Leif Karlsson's sister and the Las Vegas and the Sedona Alphas' daughters are the prized offerings. They, along with the other pack members, vow to destroy the ring.

The error I made was not issuing the command to eliminate the remaining rings soon after Blaise. We didn't expect them to jump back into operation so soon. The pause allowed them to gain control and to use Blaise and Bernard's loss to increase their reach.

Now, the Alphas of the six packs gather with their best enforcers for what will be a battle or an all-out war.

I glance around and send a silent prayer to the gods to fight beside us. A decisive nod, and we move towards the location using the surrounding trees as cover. Below the moonless night sky, our forms blend with the inky shadows. Forest creatures scurry from the path of apex predators in human and in wolf forms. Even the insects remain silent. The air crackles with electricity.

The exhilarating charge zings across my skin. The familiar sensations of a dangerous mission descend upon me. Brain sharp. Vision laser level. Muscles taut. I sniff the air to detect the enemy. Even with my keen sense of smell, they're indistinguishable from the gathered packs. However, we tied black bandanas around our necks to differentiate us from the breeding ring members.

My fingers slide from the semiautomatic trigger to test the knot on my bandana. Unconsciously, I nod at finding it secure. I have no desire to get taken out by friendly fire or fangs. Voices over my earpiece bring my finger back to the trigger. Time to kill these bastards once and for all.

"Eagle in position."

"Owl in position."

"Hawk in position."

Once the last of the six pack Alphas confirms his unit is ready, I give the word.

"Finish the fuckers!"

Amped-up yeses fill the earpieces. Then silence.

With the stealth of our kind, we converge on the location. Dolph, Colin, and the rest of our unit move towards the auction building with the goal of securing the breeding ring leaders. Around us, grunts, snapping bones, and muffled cries of pain indicate other units engaged with the ring's patrol. Undisturbed, our unit moves on.

We reach the abandoned barn. Two males flank the double doors while I take point with Dolph, as my beta, behind me. Colin, as the head enforcer, follows with the rest of the unit positioned around him. My head cocks as my ears hone in for sounds of activity inside the barn. The almost undetectable hum of low voices confirms individuals present. I nod at the two males flanking the doors. Without delay, they slide them open.

A few lanterns towards the rear cast light in the darkened interior. The hum becomes distinct voices as they drone on, seemingly unaware of our presence. No movement. I notice the words repeat as I step forward. Before I can give voice to the warning bells ringing in my head, a soft click reaches my ears. Followed by another and another still. A domino effect in seconds.

My head swivels following the sounds until a sharp whistle raises goosebumps on my skin, even as the hairs on the back of my neck rise. The only reactions I have before a blast of heat and metal from all around knocks my legs from under me.

Excruciating pain radiates through each of my limbs. The air in my lungs seizes. A scream rips from my throat. Flames lick along my exposed skin. The nauseating scent of my charred flesh fills my nostrils. As my body convulses, another string of explosives rocks the barn.

Instinctively, my wolf fights to take over and relieve me

of the intense agony. His anguished howl rises with the others until my mind shuts down, and I feel no more.

~

SIGNY

"CAREFUL! He's the worse of them."

My heart stutters at Sage's words at the same time a mate bond flares in my heart. I pivot and race from the hospital room designated for Garrett, Dolph, and Colin.

The hospital is a state-of-the-art facility with all the latest equipment, two operating rooms, and twenty patient rooms. They spared no expense to make it the best care facility for our pack. Departments include urgent care, general medicine, obstetrics, and pediatrics. A fully trained staff of three pack doctors, nurses, aides, and the head of administration run the hospital efficiently.

Even though it's rare for a wolf shifter to require medical help since we have enhanced healing, every pack has a full hospital. Accidents can require further help, and wolf shifters cannot run to a human emergency room. The risk of detection of our kind proves too great.

And the return of many severely injured Alphas and enforcers to each pack will test the hospitals and their staffs' abilities.

The realization knocks the breath from my lungs as my eyes land on the gurney being pushed by a nurse. I can't recognize the male lying still. However, a whiff of sandalwood and vanilla reaches my nostrils. I inhale deeply of the enticing scent.

"Garrett!"

The soles of my sneakers pound the tile floor as I race forward. Tears blur my vision. Shaky fingers swipe my eyes. As much as I want to curl into a fetal position and cry at the sight of my unconscious mate, I'm more determined to be strong for him. My hand reaches out—

"No!"

I jerk at Sage's sharp command. Eyes fly to hers. She shakes her head.

"Garrett isn't doing well, despite my magick," she says, eyes never leaving his bloodied face. "Let them place him in his room. I'll tell you more once he's settled."

I bite my tongue to block the cry from escaping and nod as more tears threaten to blind me. My eyes squeeze shut.

Breathe, Signy. Breath.

"Where are Dolph and Colin?" I ask as I glance down the corridor, then trail behind Sage, who follows the gurney. "You said Garrett is 'the worse of them.' Of all or of my three?"

"My sisters are bringing Dolph and Colin. They should appear soon."

I grab her arm and tug her to a stop. Her tired eyes widen.

"But are they all right? Please, Sage. Tell me!"

She places her hand over mine and squeezes.

"They're not as bad. But will need plenty of time to recover, too. Come, I sense my sisters' arrivals. Let's get Garrett settled before the other two need to be placed in their beds. Okay?"

I swallow and nod.

Gods, I beg you, please let them heal. Please!

Sage's lips move as she focuses on Garrett.

His enormous body draped in a sheet rises and floats sideways, then hovers over the bed. The nurse slides the covers to the foot of the bed. Gently, his body lowers to the mattress. I hurry forward and help lift the covers over him.

Tenderly, I brush aside the slick strands of his long, jet black hair before my eyes scan his face for any sign of distress. A red bruise outlines a gash on his forehead. Puffy eyelids hide his glacial blue eyes. Trails of dried blood dribble from his nose to the split upper lip. More blood covers the stubble on his firm jaw.

My gaze sweeps back to his closed eyes.

"Oh, Garrett, my love—"

The words catch in my throat, replaced by a sob. I continue to stare at his unresponsive form until the comforting masculine scent of Dolph permeates my mind. Colin's leather and spices mixed with his natural musk follow on my next breath. I whip around, eyes seeking my other mates.

"Easy with him!" Willow exclaims as a nurse rolls Dolph into the room.

"Him, too!" Lillie adds when the nurse with Colin bumps the gurney over the threshold.

Like Garrett, they lie unconscious, even as the twins levitate them to their beds.

I wait until they're settled, then rush from one to the other, checking their bloodied faces. I close my eyes and lean into our mate bonds, hoping to connect with them on the deeper level. Only weak pulses respond. But I'll take them as wins nonetheless, thankful they returned alive to me. And as Colin promised, he came back in one piece, albeit gravely injured.

"Signy," Sage murmurs.

I drag my gaze from Colin and face her.

"Willow and Lillie need to return for the others while I return to Jagger and our pack. But first, I'll update you and the doctors. Let's step into the corridor so their families can hear too."

Outside of their room, I stare into anxious faces as they ask Sage questions. She raises her hand, and they quiet.

"It was a setup. Only a dozen members of the ring were there and now dead. But not one she-wolf, human female, or pup. This was intentional to lure our males to the location."

Angry words rise as we curse the bastards. Sage nods and continues.

"They rigged the barn and trucks with explosives. Silver shrapnel embedded in their bodies. Garrett took the worse of it since he was in the lead when they entered the barn, followed by Dolph, then Colin."

She pauses as Idonea and Thyra cry out. Arne and

Randel embrace them as their eyes lock onto Sage. They nod, and she continues.

"Willow, Lillie, and I removed the silver. But the damage is extensive, particularly to Garrett's legs. They also suffered major burns. In Garrett's case, he partially shifted to aid with his healing. But that won't be enough, as you know silver is deadly to wolf shifters. I forced his wolf back to allow my magick to work, then put him into a coma. His body needs to focus all energy on healing."

She turns to Willow.

"Dolph had internal hemorrhaging from the impact of several projectiles. When we arrived, he was bleeding in his chest and belly cavities. I repaired his organs, increased blood production, and placed him in a coma to speed his recovery."

Lillie speaks next.

"Colin fell face first, resulting in multiple broken facial bones and a head injury. I mended the bones and reversed the injury. As a precaution, I sedated him. It will wear off after a few of days."

She turns to Sage, who nods.

"Monitor them for now. However, once Willow and Lillie return with the others, they will remain here to assist with all the injured. The others in our coven have returned the rest to their packs. Local witches will tend to them and report their progress to me. I will discuss all with the Lunas, including you, Signy, who will temporarily run the Ruling Council until the Alphas heal. We need to find the she-wolves and human females. Any questions?"

My mind spins with the extent of their injuries and with their diagnoses. Comas? We've come full circle, first me, now Garrett and Dolph. Fortunately, Lillie only sedated Colin, not that it makes his situation any less. *Gods!*

"Do you think they'll heal completely?" I ask as I glance back into their quiet room.

Sage takes a deep breath and exhales slowly as she considers her answer. My gaze returns to her.

"Our magick is powerful. We need to help heal, not replace nature's way, and cause more harm than good. We will continue in stages. So, it will take time. Stay with them. Let them know you're present."

She pulls me in for a hug.

"We must be strong, Signy, no matter what. Now, I must return to my mate and pack," she whispers.

A sob cuts into my verbal response. I hug her tightly.

Sage steps back, then the three of them disappear.

Mutely, I walk into the room and begin the first of what I imagine being many vigils over Garrett, Dolph, and Colin.

olin

"—can't take care of them if you don't eat and get some sleep, Signy. It's been three days and all you've done is move from one bedside chair to the next."

"Estrid, I appreciate your concern. Truly. But I'm fine. I ate earlier."

"Half of a bagel with cream cheese? That's not enough. What do you think Colin would say if he knew you weren't taking care of yourse—"

"He'd be beyond pissed," I mutter in a raspy voice, then blink my eyes open, searching the room for my stubborn mate. Her ice blue eyes bug from her head. I cock an eyebrow and mimic her response to my mother. *"Truly."*

I pin her with a reproachful stare as I raise up on an

elbow. My head swims. But I keep a straight face as I watch emotions play across hers. Shock widens her eyes further. Her full lips part as a gasp slips out. Relief softens her eyes before tears shimmer. Trembling hands cover her mouth, shaped in a perfect O.

My cock pulses to life at the memories of that same shape wrapped around my girth as the tip hits the back of her throat. I chuckle to myself, realizing I must be healed to go from keeling over to wanting Signy on her knees. If my mother wasn't present, I'd fulfill that fantasy right quick. Instead, I sit up and arrange the covers to hide my burgeoning erection.

"Colin! Thank the gods!"

"Oh, son!"

They leap to their feet and rush to stand on either side of my bed. Eager hands touch my face, chest, and arms as they assure themselves that I'm all right. I indulge their questions, thankful to be alive after that fuck up.

We should have checked the barn from the exterior before charging in.

The sounds of pain replace Signy and my mother's happy voices. The stench of flesh and fear overpower Signy's unique scent of the forest after a spring rain, woody and earthy, with a hint of wild honey straight from the comb. Their elated faces shimmer, replaced by orange flames spreading across the barn's straw-filled floor. I suck in a lungful of air, tasting the acrid smoke and burnt flesh on my tongue.

Fuck!

How many survived?

Garrett?

Dolph?

Damn, even Signy's brothers.

My pulse races for reasons other than sex.

I fight for another deep breath and close my eyes to banish the fear creeping in on me.

"Colin? Do you feel pain?"

"What's wrong, son?"

"I'll get the doctor."

My hand shoots out and grasps Signy's wrist.

"No! Stay," I rasp, now the one with wide eyes.

She nods as our mate bond thrums between us.

"I'll go for the doctor and get your father too," my mother offers as she slips from my bedside and closes the door behind her.

My eyes remain on my mate. She perches on the edge of the bed and entwines our fingers.

"It's okay. I understand," she whispers, then gestures to the side and opposite wall. "And look. Garrett and Dolph are here too. They're in comas but healing nicely."

I sag against the pillows and scrub a palm over my face. Damn, what a complete 180. My head swims again.

Get a grip, Voll.

I open my eyes and quirk my lips at Signy.

"I kept my promise."

The tears spill down her flushed cheeks as she nods vigorously.

"Yes, my love. You did, thank the gods!"

I grip her waist and pull her onto my lap, tucking her head beneath my chin. My eyes close as I inhale her scent, then sigh. Yes, thank the gods all three of us returned to her.

The door opens.

Doc enters followed by a nurse, my parents, and twin females. They glance at Garrett and Dolph as they hurry to my bedside.

Signy scoots away. But I wrap my arms around her and growl possessively. No way will I let her leave me. Her presence restores me like no medicine ever could. She lifts her eyes to mine, and I shake my head, issuing another growl. She sighs and leans against my chest, muttering under her breath about how I'm lucky I'm recovering. My responding chuckle gets me a side-eye, and I chuckle again.

"Obviously you feel better," Doc says with a knowing smirk. "Luna Sage and her sisters Willow and Lillie used their magick to heal you and those who survived…"

His words sober me up again. I miss the rest as my thoughts return to that night. In all our missions as Green Berets and after, we never had to contend with deadly silver. I recall the sensation of it ripping into my flesh and burning worse than the most intense fire. A shudder runs through me, jiggling Signy.

She shifts to gaze at me with concerned eyes.

I shake my head and tune back in to Doc.

He and Sage's sisters explain what happened and how they healed us.

I listen and flick my gaze to my best friends.

In comas for three days, their bodies remain still except for the rise and fall of their chests. I send prayers of thanks to the gods we made it back safe and prayers for the lost members of all six packs. Now, more than ever, I want to finish the fuckers. For good.

I set the thoughts aside for the few moments it takes Lillie to scan my body.

"You're all healed, Colin. Shift into your wolf and go for a run. Let your natural healing work with my magick. You'll feel even better," she says with a brilliant smile lighting up her emerald green eyes. "Signy, go with him. You need a break. Reconnect with your mate."

She grins knowingly and moves to check on Garrett while Willow scans Dolph.

The musky scent of Signy's arousal wafts up to tease my senses. She squirms in my lap. Her round ass rubs my cock, sparking it back to life. So focused on her, I barely hear my parents and the others say their good nights as erotic energy zips between my mate and me. I squeeze her hip.

"Come."

Her pupils dilate to engulf the ice blue irises, leaving only a ring at the edges. Her little pink tongue darts out to moisten her lips as she nods, then hops to her feet.

I spring from the bed, scoop her into my arms, and stride from the room, not caring my ass hangs out the back of my hospital gown. My long legs make quick work of the distance to freedom. Once outside, I jog to the edge of the forest and lower Signy to her feet, then lean down to murmur in her ear.

"Run."

Her cheeks flush darker as her eyes glitter. Without a backward glance, she races deeper into the tree line. I throw my head back and howl. Then give chase.

SIGNY

MY HEART POUNDS in my chest as my lithe legs pump faster and faster, increasing the distance between Colin and me. I don't dare to look over my shoulder and risk my footing. No. Better to keep sprinting through the forest.

"Shift!"

At Colin's powerful command, my legs stop, and I drop to my hands and knees as my ebony black wolf with a white patch on her back emerges at his dominance. Crackling and realigning of bones lengthening amidst a flash find me on all four paws in the underbrush within moments. My wolf turns her head, seeking our fated mate.

He struts naked from behind a tree. Amber eyes flash burnished gold in the moonlight. He runs a hand through the tawny longer strands atop his head and cups the buzzed sides as he cracks his neck left and right. The corded muscles of his forearms flex.

My lust-filled gaze caresses his tattoo-covered body. Broad chest with chiseled pecs I rest my cheek on. A ladder of eight-pack abs bracketed by lickable V-cuts ripple as he crouches using his thick thighs and sculpted calves. As sexy as he is, it's his ginormous cock I drool over.

Platinum beads of the deep shaft reverse Prince Albert piercing gleam in the moonlight. The plum-shaped tip an angry red and shiny with pre-cum points straight at me. My tongue lolls from my slack mouth.

"Oh, Little Wolf. You want a taste?" He chuckles wickedly. "You will have it, and I will fuck you. But first, we run as wolves."

His feral eyes never leave mine as he shifts into his tawny wolf. At six feet, eight inches, he towers over me by eleven inches in human form. As a wolf, he's a giant. And my wolf loves it.

She yips and darts forward to nip his shoulder, then scrambles away to race further into the forest. He growls deep in his chest and gives chase.

We run for hours around Moen Island. The exhilaration of being with my mate after the tragedy frees some of the worry of the last few days. For the moment, we leave it behind and romp around letting our wolves take the lead in the most primal way. Hunting, then drinking from a stream. Howling in a song. Playing until Colin's wolf nips my flank and urges my wolf towards our mansion.

We burst through the tree line into the backyard. Our claws scrabble on the flagstone patio as we pass the swimming pool surrounded by chaise lounges and an outdoor kitchen and living room. We pause at the side door.

A dramatic carving of a wolf etched in the wood welcomes us. Colin slaps his paw on a panel, and the door swings open. He lopes inside, and I follow. The door swings closed behind us automatically.

We shift, and my eyes drop to Colin's dick, knowing it'll be erect as always after we run as wolves. It doesn't disappoint. Long and thick with the platinum beads ready to stroke my most-sensitive spots. I shudder with carnal desire.

"Oh, Little Wolf, I'm ready for you, too," Colin says in a low and husky growl. "Upstairs. Now."

A mewl slips from my mouth as he slaps my ass. I skip forward and dash for the stairs and to my favorite spot in our home—our playroom.

Who knew I'm a sub and quiver at my mates being my Doms?

I know about the BDSM lifestyle since Viggo created Club Sol & Mani Miami—one of six exclusive luxury members only BDSM clubs for wolf shifters. The South Beach location is the flagship with the other five in the remaining territories. Each pack runs their club under the direction of Viggo since they're a part of the Larson Enterprises' properties division he heads.

Garrett suspected I'm a sub from our encounters at The Fortress. I complied with his commands without hesitancy. Accepted his control of my body—when I'd cum, pushing my limits. It wasn't until they claimed me that they explain my innate behavior and my pleasure found in our power exchange. They converted one room in our mansion into a pleasure den, and we delved right in to my training.

As I near the double doors, I still my thoughts to transition into the sub mindset. Give control to my Dom and gain relaxation, safety, and calmness. The scent of leather and spices mixed with his natural musk envelops me as he steps behind me.

"Come, Little Wolf," he rumbles as he opens the doors.

The melodic thrum of sensual music filters through hidden speakers. It glides over my skin like a caress as he scans my body while I pass him. He licks his lips appreciatively.

Those on my face press together as my lower lips ripple with need. The musky scent of my arousal wafts around us with each step I take.

"Ah, ah, ah," he chastises as he places his hands on tops of my shoulders from behind with downward pressure. "On your hands and knees, ass high, head low. Crawl to the spanking bench over there."

Without hesitating, I lower to position gracefully, eager to please My Dom. The deep ruby silk on silk carpet cushions my knees. A growl from behind encourages me to add an extra oomph to my movements. A pat to my bouncing ass rewards my efforts.

"Good girl, Little Wolf. You please me with your natural poise," he croons. "A true submissive."

I preen at his praise, then through my lowered eyelashes, I survey our playroom.

They designed it with me in mind and used various hues of my favorite color pink. Set in the middle of the suite is a massive, custom rose wood bed with four posters and a rose gold lattice canopy rings hang; ruby red silk sheets, duvet, and various sized pillows with a white cashmere blanket draped over the foot; from the rose wood tray ceiling, along with the Swarovski crystal chandelier and recessed lights, hang hooks; the walls and ceiling panels covered in dusty pink silk damask; drawers of an antique armoire filled with anal plugs, clamps, cords, cuffs, vibrators, and more; a spanking bench and a Sybian saddle stand on the wall opposite the armoire; on another wall sits a tantric chaise with rose gold rings; before another stands a St. Andrew's Cross; one door next to the armoire leads to the pale pink Carrara marble bathroom that has a walk-in shower for six, an oversized soaking tub, double vanities, and a separate water closet for the bidet and toilet. It's pure decadence.

I stop at the spanking bench and await his next command.

He crouches beside me and extends his hand. Eyes lowered but staring at his cock, I accept his help and rise. An ease from years of experience allows him to position then strap me to the pink sapphire leather padded bench quickly. Once he secures my ankles in the suede-lined leather restraints, My Dom strides to my head and squats to encase my wrists. As he rises to his full height, his massive girth aligns with my vision.

Yes, please!

He chuckles wickedly in response to my tongue darting out to lick my lips hungrily.

"Would you like a taste now, Little Wolf?" He asks as he strokes his length.

His dick twitches, and I moan.

Did I say, yes? I mean, hell to the yes, yes, *yes!*

Greedily, I stick my tongue out like a snake to savor the air full of his musky, masculine odor. I whine at the sight of his thick fingers wrapping around his length. He covers his dick and strokes it from root to mushroom tip. His Prince Albert piercing's balls jewelry glint in the low light.

"Do you deserve to suck my cock, Little Wolf?" He asks as he tugs his turgid staff. Veins run along its surface. Velvet covered steel.

"Yes, Sir… I promise to be good," I purr.

My Dom taps his bulbous cock head against my lips. One thrust, and he's at the back of my throat, heading south.

Gag reflex kicks in, but I fight it off with a deep breath through my nose.

"Ah, yes, Little Wolf, your promise holds true," My Dom grunts as he falls into a rhythm.

His hips snap back and forth—in deep and fast, out slow to the tip. The girth stretches my mouth, and the platinum balls stroke the roof of my mouth as he glides over my willing tongue. Soon my jaw aches and drool spills from the corners onto the bench.

"You will suck me, Little Wolf. Every. Single. Inch," he hisses. "Suck. Me. Well."

His hands grip the back of my head to hold me still as he plunders my throat. One last thrust, and his dick hardens further as it swells with his semen. Copious amounts spill down my throat in spurts as My Dom fills my belly.

I moan around his girth. My pussy creams.

His grunts and groans end as his body shudders from his toe-curling release. My Dom strokes my scalp to soothe the pain from his tugs on my hair.

So damn worth it!

His cock pops from my mouth. A shiny string of saliva connects us until he strides around to my rear.

I tremble in anticipation.

Pressure to my soaked slit makes me yelp.

"All of this wetness from you blowing me, Little Wolf?" He asks as he rubs the tip of his nose from my puckered hole to my engorged clit. On an inhale he continues, "Mmm mmm such a delectable aroma. Shall I have a taste, too?"

My whimpered response makes him chuckle. I buck against his mouth as he laps at my seam.

Oh. Oh. *Fuuuck!*

My mind takes a moment to catch up to the pain that replaces the pleasure. My globes jiggle under a flogger as its suede fringes smack my exposed ass. I grip the legs of the spanking bench as I jerk from the unexpected spanking.

"What was your first lesson in BDSM play, Little Wolf?" My Dom thunders between strikes.

I gulp and wrack my brain for the answer. My delayed response results in another volley of well-aimed smacks to the spot where the bottom curve of my butt meets thighs.

Fuuuck!

"Hold my position no matter what unless I want to safeword," I cry out in anguish as I still my body despite the flogger's fury.

Immediately he drops the offensive implement, drops to his knees, and laps at my slick inner thighs where my juices pour from my throbbing pussy. Grunts and growls fill the playroom as he feasts on my essence.

When my legs tremble from holding back my orgasm, My Dom returns to my punishment. His renewed efforts force me back from the edge even as they bring me closer to the orgasm of life.

I clench my eyes shut and my fists around the legs of the bench as I try to rein in my impending release.

"Aaaahhh.... Sssir... I... I... *Please!*" I beg when the sensation threatens to topple me over the edge.

The flogger hits the floor with a clatter again. My Dom grips my hips and slams home. He's so deep I can feel the balls of his piercing brush my cervix.

We groan in unison.

"*Yeeesss, Sir!*" I scream in the throes of erotic ecstasy.

"Whose pussy is this?!"

"Yours!" I wail as I lose myself to the bliss of subspace and the joy of having one of my mates awake. Our connection is strong again.

My last thought is of Garrett and Dolph.

Awake for me, my loves.

CHAPTER 6

olph

"You're ready to wake up now, Dolph."

Warmth collects in my chest and radiates outward, infusing every cell of my body with energy. Behind my closed eyes, I watch the energy expand like a supernova, tendrils reaching from the core until it bursts.

On a gasp, my eyelids fly open as I sit up straight. Emerald green eyes glowing with power meet my gaze.

"Who are you?"

A smile spreads across her face as she lowers her hands. I swear swirls of blue light glimmer from her fingertips. A blink, and they disappear. A witch? Where the hell am I?

The dark forest. Male wolf shifters in combat gear stalk through the trees. Garrett crumpling to the barn floor.

Reaching for him. Excruciating pain in my torso. Screams. My screams. Blood. So. Much. Blood.

My head jerks.

I glance around as my hands pat my chest and belly, certain to find silver shrapnel embedded in my flesh. My wild eyes land on Signy. Hers shine with unshed tears.

Another surge in my chest. This time from the flare of our mate bond reengaging. My fist presses against my heart. I felt it shred that night. Now, it beats anew, and our bond ignites again.

"Dolph, it's all right, my love. You're safe in the hospital on Moen Island," she says, stepping forward, drawing my eyes to Colin beside her. He nods as she continues. "Sage and her sisters, along with several witches from their coven, rescued the three of you and so many others. They used their magick to transport you home and heal you."

She gestures towards the witch with the emerald green eyes.

"I'm Willow Waters," she says. "Your body is healthy. How is your mind?"

My only thought is to have my mate back in my arms. I stand and wrap my larger body around her smaller one, melding us together. My face burrows into her silky ebony black hair. At last, I relax as I lose myself in the forest after a spring rain, woody and earthy, with a hint of wild honey straight from the comb that is my Signy. I inhale deeply and squeeze her tighter.

"Gods. I didn't think I'd see you in this life again."

"Oh, Dolph. I thank the gods every waking moment for your return."

She lifts her face to stare up at me.

"But answer Willow. We need to be sure you're completely healed like Colin."

Without loosening my hold on her, I nod and look over the top of her head at Willow.

"My mind is as strong as ever. Thank you for saving us," I respond, then shift my gaze to Garrett unconscious in bed. "How is he?"

With Signy tucked against my side, I make my way to his bed. Colin flanks me as we stare at our best friend, commander, and Alpha. Knowing the witches used their magick on him lessens the worry. But I saw him fall that night and being the only one of us still out of it concerns me.

I listen as Willow recounts his injuries and magickal treatment. My eyes move to his motionless legs beneath the covers. *Gods, let him walk again.*

"Today's scan of his body confirms he's healing, but just needs more time. As you know, Alphas are stronger than other wolf shifters. So, a few more days should be enough," she says and inclines her head at Colin and me. "The two of you had grave injuries—broken face and shredded organs, hemorrhaging. You're fine. Garrett will recover too. Now, go run as your wolf for a dose of your enhanced healing."

"It worked wonders for me," Colin smirks as he winks at Signy.

I glance between the two of them. Her cheeks pinken as

her eyes lower. Huh. I cock an eyebrow at Colin, and his grin widens.

"I'm going to read a story to our boy here. You two go for a long and hard *run*. Get your juices flowing. Nothing compares to that type of healing."

He chuckles as he sits on the chair next to Garrett's bed and picks up a book from the side table.

Willow giggles and heads for the door.

I glance down at Signy.

"Let's go."

She peeks at me from beneath the thick fringe of her eyelashes as her teeth catch the corner of her lower lip. Pink cheeks heat crimson as she nods.

Yeah, this will be the best medicine. The ultimate cure-all.

I brush my lips over the top of Signy's head as I move us towards the door, hugging her close. As much as I want to race for the exit, I shorten my steps so she can keep pace with me. At almost a foot shorter, her legs are no match for mine.

My golden wolf paces on the periphery of my mind, ready to run free. I'm just as eager to flex my muscles. Leave the darkness of that night behind. My responsibility to our pack comes to the forefront with Garrett temporarily incapacitated. As his beta and Moen, Inc. COO, I'm next in line to run our pack and our company.

But as I open the hospital doors, fresh air fills my lungs, and the sun warms my skin exposed by the hospital gown. I push those thoughts aside.

"Time to run, mate."

She scoots from under my arm and dashes for the forest. Ass swaying like a red flag.

I throw my head back and howl before I give chase. Mid stride, my wolf breaks free, landing on four massive paws without missing a step. The shredded gown drops to the grass as I follow her.

Time passes quickly as we race across the acres of pristine forest. My strength increases with each minute in wolf form. But my cock aches to plunge into Signy's sweet pussy. I will not suppress my carnal urge any longer.

She prances around me, bounding in and out of reach. On her next pass, I lunge and grip the scruff of her neck between my jaws, then shake my head. She yelps and drops to her haunches.

Attention captured, I bark and take off for the cabin where we claimed her. With a yip, she follows. The beauty of the forest passes in a blur until we reach the clearing.

In the center stands the rugged cabin. A great room with furniture and the kitchen with a dining table. One bedroom with a massive bed and a bathroom. I charge towards the front door, Signy at my side.

We shift on the porch. She enters ahead of me.

Mesmerized by her supple, naked body, I prowl towards her. She senses my carnal lust through our mate bond and pivots. The wolf and the she-wolf face off. I growl as I pull her into my arms and cover her mouth with mine.

She melds her soft body against my hard, muscular

frame. A purr vibrates from between her kiss-swollen lips when I suck on her tongue.

"Tell me. What do you want?" I growl.

"You, Dolph. Only you," she breathes.

I sweep her from her feet and carry her to the bedroom. My heart pounds with each step. Without a doubt, she must feel its rapid beat against her tits.

Beside the massive bed, I let her slide down my body until she lands on her feet. My hands glide along her flanks to rest at her hips. Once again, I devour her mouth. Her hungry moans spur me on. My fingers dig into the soft flesh.

"I want you. I crave you, Little Wolf," I utter in a hoarse whisper, barely audible.

She shudders. Her tits jiggle against my chest.

"Please," she cries.

No time for role play tonight. I want to bury myself balls deep within her. I scoop her up and toss her onto the middle of the bed. Arms and legs flail until she bounces amongst the mounds of pillows she added to *soften up the room.*

Bared before me, Signy takes my breath away.

Luscious full tits tipped with rosy pink distended nipples make my mouth water. The flat expanse of her belly leads to a smooth mound. Pussy lips drip with her juices as her engorged clit peeks from between them. A narrow waist leads to grip-worthy hips. Long, toned legs beg to wrap around my hips and lock at the slim ankles. Even the pearly pink polish on her toenails calls to me.

Mine!

The mattress dips as I kneel my way to plank above her. Forearms frame her gorgeous face before I take her mouth in a savage kiss to possess her once and for all. The searing kiss ends, and I nip, lick, and suck my way down her throat. I lap at my claiming bite.

She shivers and moans.

The erotic sound shoots to my throbbing cock. My head dips to one plump nipple. I engulf it. Then suckle. Hard.

She groans from the pain-tinged pleasure and bows her back. Pushing her tit deeper into my hungry mouth.

I want to fuck her until I can't walk. Until I'm blinded by my orgasm, and I pass out.

My Little Wolf must sense my need and reaches for my rock-hard cock thumping against my eight-pack abs.

Pre-cum dribbles from its purple tip.

"Oh gods, how I've missed you," she pants. "I—I was so afraid I lost all of you."

"Never!" I growl as the rumble deep in my chest seeks to soothe her.

My mouth descends on hers as the rumbling continues. I possess every inch of her mouth until she writhes beneath me, tilting her pelvis to notch my cock to her soaked slit.

I sit back on my haunches. She pouts as my dick slips from her little hand. With a smirk, I grasp her ankles.

"Spread your legs for me, baby."

They fall open to reveal her engorged clit and the glistening pink petals of her pussy. Her juices coat her inner thighs.

I descend on her bounty, like the feral beast I am.

My tongue, teeth, and fingers coax three orgasms from her before I deem her ready to take my length and girth. I want her sore from my fucking. But not in pain.

I kiss my way up her body until our mouths meet again. I make her taste her sweet pussy juices still fresh in my mouth as I drive my tongue between her slack lips.

She moans and sucks the musky flavor. I groan as my cock jerks.

My hips settle between her thighs. I take a moment to etch on my memory her face flushed with erotic pleasure. I brush my lips against hers as I cradle her head with my palms. Otherwise, my first thrust will send her flying towards the headboard. I. Want. Her. Bad.

My tip aligns with her pussy.

"Open up and let me in," I command. "Take my dick like a good girl."

Her entire body shudders as she moans.

I surge forward with a snap of my hips.

One thrust impales her on my dick.

She wails at the massive invasion.

My hips still to allow her pussy to adjust to my size. I cover her face and mouth with hungry kisses to urge her body to accept me.

The soft yielding of her core intoxicates me.

I shift position to lower my hands beneath her round

ass. Each one grasps a butt cheek to hold her steady for the impending fucking.

"Look at me, Signy," I growl. "I want to see your eyes as you cum all over my giant cock. Do not look away for a second."

She whimpers. But her hooded eyes focus on mine. Pupils blown with lust.

My hips draw back until only my tip breaches her pussy. Then I ram my dick forward to the very end of her core. The sensation of possessing her fully makes my eyes roll back in my head.

A long, low groan falls from my slack mouth.

"Fuuuck... You feel so good. So... tight... So wet," I rasp.

"*Oh gods, Dolph...* Oooh..." she wails and stiffens.

The first flutter of her pussy along my length signals her fourth orgasm. Her inner walls clamp down on my cock in a vise-like grip.

I grunt and begin to piston my hungry cock in and out of her creamy core. Time stands still as my dick stretches and fills her tight pussy. I open my eyes to stare down at her as my fingers dig into her ass to hold her just right.

"I can feel how you respond to me. So willing and so soaking wet," I grunt between thrusts. "Fuck me like you miss me."

She shudders and cries out in wild abandon as another orgasm rips through her quivering pussy.

"*Yesss!*" I roar as I pummel her again and again, chasing a mind-blowing release.

My knees dig into the mattress to gain purchase. One

hand lifts to grip the back of her neck and lift her torso to my chest. Her waist-length hair falls around us like a curtain as she her fingernails dig into my shoulders. My pelvis punches up as I yank her down.

Deeper.

Deeper.

Deeper.

"Unh… Unh… Unh…" I grunt.

A zing races along my spine. My heavy balls draw up.

When my release is upon me, I throw my head back and roar.

"*Mine!*"

CHAPTER 7

olph

"I DON'T HATE TO INTERRUPT."

One eye cracks open to find Colin standing beside our bed in the mansion. The silk sheet lifts, uncovering Signy, still asleep, draped over my chest with a knee between my thighs. One hand palms her ass while the other holds her arm against my shoulder.

After our run and fucking at the cabin, we returned home. Colin stayed with Garrett to give us time to reconnect. Obviously, that time has ended.

I grumble as he crawls in behind her. He shrugs remorselessly and nuzzles her neck.

"Wake up, Sunshine. Your mate has need of another *run.*"

My dick twitches.

Yeah, a *run* sounds right.

I shift to my elbow, sliding Signy from my chest. She mumbles my name as she reaches for me. I grin at Colin, who rolls his eyes.

"She'll know I'm here once my fat cock plunders her sweet pussy. She'll wake screaming *my* name."

I chuckle and turn my attention to our mate. Her rosy cheeks and kiss-swollen lips aren't the only evidence I rode her hard all night. My fingers reach between us to cup her plump pussy lips, still slick from her juices and my cum. The combination leaks down her thighs. I use it to coat my fingertips as I swirl them over her engorged clit.

A throaty moan slips from her parted lips as her hips move to follow my circles. My fingertips move faster, urging an orgasm from her pussy. Eyes still closed, she pants as the pressure builds.

Not to be outdone, Colin scoots down her back, trailing kisses until his mouth reaches her pussy. His hands grip her hips and arch her pelvis backwards. My fingertips follow, not moving from her throbbing clit.

Obscene wet noises fill the air along with the musky scent of her arousal as he nips, sucks, and laves her pussy. She writhes, spreading her legs to give us better access. Cries of passion fall from her mouth as her cheeks redden.

"Cum for us. Cum for your mates," I demand, thumb and forefinger squeezing her clit. A tug, and she explodes, gushing into my palm and into Colin's mouth. "Fuck yes, good girl!"

I stare down into her heavy-lidded eyes before my mouth crashes onto hers for a savage kiss.

Colin's knee bumps my thigh as he slides up behind her. Her mouth tears from mine.

"Fuck, Colin!"

I glance over her head to find a satisfied grin spreading across his face. Mouth and stubble shiny from her juices. He smacks his lips lewdly and winks at me as the front of her body smacks into mine from his brutal thrusts. Full tits bounce against my chest. I cock an eyebrow and lift her top leg, opening her up to me.

Two can play this game.

I grip the base of my rock-hard cock. Catching his rhythm, I wait to thrust into her pussy as he pulls back to his tip. Her pussy lips spread around his cock, not wanting to let it go. Mine weeps enviously. Our dicks are huge. But the gods made our fated mate for us. She'll take every single inch of both. And love it.

Fully awake and doubly penetrated, she scrabbles at my shoulders. Nails embed crescent moons in my skin as she holds on. Her gasps and mewls join our grunts. Her pussy walls choke my dick as another orgasm rips through her core. Head thrown back, eyes squeezed shut, she keens.

"Oh... *Yeesss.* So... damn... good..."

"You like two giant dicks deep in your tight, little hole? Fucking you hard? Making you cum again and again?"

"Gods, yes, Colin!"

"Then. Fucking. Take. Them."

Our cocks rub as he punctuates each word with a thrust.

The sensation of her tight, juicy pussy with his thick, hard dick on mine fills my heavy balls. I plant a hand beside her head and drag her thigh over my shoulder. Spread wide, I slam my cock deeper into her pussy, barking her name as the tip hits her womb.

The sudden urge to breed our mate fills my head. Not like those monsters. No. Our mate with our pups.

Visions of her belly round with our pups dance before my eyes, along with sparks of white light. Tantalizing tits full of milk. Nipples plump and ready to suckle…

"Dolph!"

She screams my name as she cums hard. Legs shake uncontrollably. Back bows. Fingernails dig deeper. Her head lolls.

Colin catches her chin with his fingers to tilt her head towards him. His mouth descends on hers with a hungry growl as his hips piston without missing our rhythm.

My sweat drips onto her bouncing tits. I lean over and lap at it, then engulf a tit, flicking my tongue over the distended tip. Teeth graze it, then nip.

She bucks with another wail.

I continue to suckle as though her milk flows freely. But the need to cum wins.

"I'm going to fill your womb with my seed, mate. Ready for me to give it to you?" I growl.

She nods her head as she moans, full of our dicks.

"Oh, Little Wolf, we're gonna blow our loads so deep,

your little pussy will drip for days," Colin snarls barbarically.

He smacks her ass three times in quick succession. She yelps. Her pussy walls tighten around our cocks. We bellow in unison as the increased pressure triggers mind-numbing climaxes.

My eyes roll back as unimaginable pleasure zings down my spine, straight to my balls.

Copious amounts of hot, creamy cum erupt from our tips straight into her womb. Her walls convulse along our lengths, milking us of every drop. Our strangled cries fill the room. The heady scent of sex hangs heavy in the air.

Signy lays limp between us. Our thrusts slow down to a lazy pace, alternating in and out of her well-worn pussy. It ripples with aftershocks of her orgasm.

I press a gentle kiss against her sweat-drenched hair before my cock slips from her pussy. Hot, I collapse onto my back and close my eyes. Colin murmurs something to her before he falls back onto the bed. She sighs in carnal bliss and burrows into the sheets.

My thoughts return to pups.

That night was the closest we've ever come to dying. Gone forever in moments. I don't know about Garrett and Colin. But it must explain my need to put pups in Signy. Continue our line. Our future.

The idea grows in my mind as I drift to sleep.

"Rise and shine, cupcake."

One eye cracks open to find Colin sitting up with Signy on his lap. My morning wood tents the sheet draped across my hips. He smirks. Signy bites her lower lip. I roll to my side and reach for her, only to have him switch her to his other leg.

"What the fuck?" I growl, sitting up, arms outstretched for her.

Both shake their heads. My eyebrows lift to my hairline. *The hell?*

Signy smiles softly and entwines our fingers.

"We need to talk before my visit with Garrett. It's what I did with each of you before you awoke. My time to connect with you, even though you were in comas. By not have you fully, the alone time made my sadness a bit more bearable," she says then squeezes my fingers. "I hope you understand. And I'll make it up to you later, I promise, my love."

I kiss her fingertips and smile at her, then shift my gaze to glare at Colin.

"I understand, baby. But why does he get to hold you?" I grumble.

"The early wolf gets the babe," Colin says with a smirk and wraps his arms tighter around Signy.

"Fuck off."

"Now, now. We share, remember?" She says as she slips from Colin's lap and settles in the space between the two of us. "Better?"

I grin and nod while Colin flares his nostrils.

"Much. Talk to me, baby," I say, placing a possessive hand on one of her thighs and ignoring Colin doing the same.

She takes a deep breath.

"Now, you're out of the coma, Dolph. Are you ready to take over as pack beta and run Moen, Inc. as COO until Garrett awakes? I want to spend more time with him and less time being Luna and helping Randel. Every day, I pray the gods will rejoin us so we can have our happily ever after and have it last forever. Encourage him to heal faster and join us again…"

A sob catches in her throat as tears shine in her ice blue eyes.

"Please don't cry, baby," I say as I cup her cheek, rubbing my thumb on the soft skin.

"We will, Little Wolf," Colin adds, nuzzling his claiming bite.

She nods and continues, "We've lost so much time from the start when I didn't know who and what I was and some of us didn't acknowledge us being fated mates, including me when I left you. Then the brief moment we had after you claimed me evaporated like dew in the Everglades as the sun rises. The two of you healed already. But Garrett. I need to be with him and let him know he's on my mind, never forgotten…"

Her words trail off as she covers her face with trembling hands.

I wrap an arm around her shaking shoulders and bury my face in her hair. Colin loops his arms around her waist, kissing her temple. We rumble in our chests to soothe our mate's distress. A few moments pass before her sobs lessen.

I realize how brave she's been and held her pain inside

to focus on us and on the pack. Our strong, little mate needs us more than I realize. Now more than ever, her happiness must top all.

"Oh, baby. We're so proud of you for taking on your role as Luna and caring for the pack and the company despite worrying about us. You don't have to do it anymore. Colin and I will meet with the pack, then go to the headquarters in the city. When we get back, we'll have dinner in Garrett's hospital room, our foursome."

"Yeah. And maybe the aroma will entice him to wake the hell up already," Colin adds, chuckling. "We love you, Little Wolf, and want you happy."

She whispers words of thanks.

Then an idea pops into my head. I grasp her left hand and tap her empty ring finger. My eyes lift to hers. They widen.

"We issued our claiming bites. But we haven't had our mate bonding ceremony. Why don't we set the date?"

"Right! You focus on planning our ceremony and the future we'll have together. It'll be therapeutic for you," Colin says, threading his fingers with her right hand.

Signy throws her arms around our necks and hugs us close.

"What a wonderful idea! Willow says Garrett should be awake soon. We can set the date a month from now. Give me time to organize everything and for the other Alphas to be healed and able to attend. I can't wait to tell my girls and our moms!"

She grasps my face and kisses me, then does the same to Colin before she leaps from the bed.

"But first, I have to tell Garrett!"

We watch as she dashes to the en suite bathroom. Once the door closes, I turn to Colin.

"I don't want to upset Signy. But we have to check with Thyra about any chatter on the breeding rings and meet with the Ruling Council. This shit isn't over yet."

igny

"OH, Garrett, I can't wait for you to wake up. I miss you, my love. Everyone misses you. I spoke with Dolph and Colin earlier. I don't mind being responsible for our pack and Moen, Inc. But I asked Dolph if he's well enough to take over. Thank the gods he is. He also suggested we set the date for our mate bonding ceremony, and that I focus on planning it instead of the pack and Moen. I'm so excited!"

I continue massaging his legs as I fill him in on my thoughts for the ceremony. It's our time to be alone for a couple of hours after I eat breakfast.

Two days passed since Dolph awoke. It's been incredible with him and with Colin. They're back to their full strength and are even more virile than before. They fuck me like it's their mission to imprint their essence on me. My pussy softens and drips juices onto the gusset of my silk thong, just recalling their intense passion. I close my eyes and allow the wave of carnal pleasure to sweep over me. Responding pulses across their mate bonds stroke my heart like their thick cocks plundered my pussy.

Tandem fucking is oh so satisfying... But a trio of ravenous Alpha males? Erotic sin.

I open my eyes and recall our escapades to Garrett. Perhaps knowing he's missing all the fun will motivate him to wake from the magick-induced coma early. My hands move higher up his thighs until my fingertips brush his balls sac.

Instantly, his massive cock thickens and lengthens.

My mouth waters as it rises like a flagpole straight into the air. Lickable veins and ridges line the shaft. The plum-shaped tip darkens. I swallow, then glance over my shoulder at the closed door. Since the hospital staff won't disturb my visits, my tongue slips out to moisten my lips, and I climb onto the bed.

Why should Garrett miss any pleasure?

Straddling his calves, I brace my hands on either side of his narrow hips and lean over. The tip of my tongue laps the bead of pre-cum glistening at the slit. I hum at the back of my throat as the salty flavor bursts across my tastebuds.

My eyes close in ecstasy. My pussy tingles.

"You taste divine, my love," I murmur as my lips rub

around his tip, smearing it with more pre-cum. "You miss me, too?"

As though answering my question, his cock bobs yes.

I laugh lustily and lave the underside from root to tip with the flat of my tongue. It swirls around, collecting more of his cream. I purr like a cat and clench my pussy. I set my need aside and treat his cock like my favorite lollipop.

My mouth engulfs the bulbous head as my hand fists the base. It's so thick, my fingertips don't meet. I give it a squeeze and fist up as my mouth lowers down. My gag reflex kicks in when his tip taps the back of my throat. I pull up on a gasp and breathe.

Cupping his sac with my other hand, I massage his balls. My mouth returns to his length to meet my fist, then draws back to suck on the head. Both hands squeeze, and I'm rewarded with a dribble of pre-cum. Hungrily, I lap it up. My moan vibrates along his cock. It thumps against the roof of my mouth. I relax my throat and inhale through my nose to take him deep. My eyes water from my effort.

Slowly, I pull up. My warm breath blows across his cock, wet with my saliva. I groan at the sight of the veins thickening as he grows even bigger. My clit pulses with equal need.

I slip a hand between my legs. Fingers slip beneath the soaked thong. I mewl as they brush past my swollen pussy lips and tap the tip of my clit. My thighs wobble.

"Oh, *gods*, Garrett."

A mini orgasm ripples through my pussy. I shudder and

give myself a moment before my mouth returns to his dick. I cry out around his girth as more of his musky essence leaks onto my tongue. The bobbing of my head matches the circling of my clit as I work to bring us both to climax. His enticing sandalwood and vanilla scent mixes with our musky arousal. The erotic sounds of my wet mouth on his cock match the slickness of my pussy.

My cheeks hallow out. His cock grows impossibly larger. My hips gyrate. Fingers tangle in my hair. Hips pump up. I cry out in surprise, loosening my hold on his cock.

"*Grrrr…* Do. Not. Fucking. Stop!"

Garrett tightens his hold on the back of my head and pistons his hips. My pussy gushes from his passionate dominance. His primal grunts increase as he plunders my mouth. His cock slides down my throat. I choke as tears slip down my cheeks and my lips press against his groin.

"*Fuuuck, Signy!*"

His roar punches the air as his dick pulses on my tongue. Like a geyser, it spurts in a series of powerful spasms down my stretched throat. His thick, milky seed shoots straight into my belly.

My fingers pinch my slippery clit. Stars dance against the backdrop of my closed eyelids. I cry out around his massive girth, panting and choking for air. His hips drop to the bed, and his cock pops from my mouth.

"Oh, baby, did I miss you too," he growls as he hoists me over his body.

Hands cup my ass, pressing my pelvis against his still

erect dick. Between ragged breaths, he feathers kisses along my throat, ending with a kiss to his claiming bite.

I shudder from a tremor in my pussy. Breathless and sated, I burrow my face into his long hair. My heart races as much from the epic blowjob as from Garrett being awake at last. Tears of joy drip into his hair.

"Hush, My Queen. I heard all you shared with me from the moment I arrived. You do not know how badly I wanted to respond but could not," he murmurs as he strokes my back. "The witches were right. My body needed time to heal. The gods bless them for saving me and so many others. We are indebted to Luna Sage and her covens. Jagger is a lucky male to have such a powerful and caring mate."

I nod, recalling my conversation with my brothers a couple of days ago. Fully healed and more concerned about me than themselves. I will never forget what Sage and the witches did for us.

"Now, I know how Sleeping Beauty felt," Garrett chuckles. "But your kiss blows away the peck her prince gave her."

I giggle and rise to my elbows, staring down at his handsome face. Glacial blue eyes sparkle above full lips quirked into a grin.

"You prove too irresistible, my love. I just hope I didn't creep you out sucking your dick while in a coma."

Arousal darkens his eyes to cobalt blue. They flash electric with his wolf close to the surface. He undulates his hips, gripping fistfuls of my ass.

"You can creep all over me any day, My Queen," he rumbles. "Now, it's my turn."

Swiftly, he flips us over. I gasp and cling to his bulging biceps. Legs lock around his hips instinctively. He reaches between us to rip the ruined silk thong off. I whimper when it pinches my sensitive clit. Garrett's fingers tease the bite of pain away, then thrust between my soaked folds. My moan morphs into a strangled cry when his thick cock plunges balls deep.

He rides me hard and fast. Between thrusts, he lowers his head and laps at my left nipple. Then brings his lips to lick at my mouth voraciously. My lips part, giving him full access for our tongues to tangle. He swallows my passionate cries, even as his groans vibrate between us.

"Hold on to my waist," he rasps as he rises above me and grips the headboard.

His eyes flash electric blue as he drills me into the mattress.

"You like how my big cock claims every inch of your pussy, Little Wolf?"

My mouth opens in a wordless cry.

"Then take what I give you until you squeeze my seed straight into your womb. You. Are. Mine!"

My eyes roll back as a mind-shattering orgasm hurtles through me, robbing me of not only my mind, but my body and my very soul. Incapacitated, I collapse limp while Garrett chases his release like a wild beast. Another orgasm overtakes me as he bottoms out and floods my pussy with his hot cum.

He drops heavily on top of me, and I welcome his weight with a blissful sigh as I drift asleep.

"I love you, Signy," he murmurs, voice hoarse, barely audible.

Hours later, I'm still floating on Cloud Garrett as I sit on a sofa in my office having just shared him awaking—not by my *kiss*—and our upcoming mate bonding ceremony.

"Oh, honey! That's fabulous news!"

"Just what we need to bring a bit of joy to the packs."

"Marvelous! Let me put my event planner hat on."

My grin stretches from ear to ear as I listen to my mother and my girls exclaim congratulations and clap. Their happy faces fill the flat-screen television mounted on the wall.

My mothers-in-law, Thyra, and Vera join me in the sitting area. A tray of tea and cookies rests on the coffee table between the sofas. I pop a sugar cookie into my mouth as I shimmy in my seat.

"I know right!" I say around swallowing. Hey, a girl gets good with her mouth.

"Tell us your vision," my mother Sigrid says.

I explain my desire to have the mate bonding ceremony with elements from a traditional wedding. After all, I am the Miami Pack Princess and now the New York Wolves Queen. It's my chance to have the day of my dreams. While I go into details, Wren taps away on her tablet, asking questions as I go.

Before long, we have a four-day affair planned inviting family, friends, pack Alphas and betas with their mates, and the witches who saved them. Everyone will arrive on Friday morning. Family staying in guest houses on Moen Island and friends, other packs, and the witches taking over a luxury bed-and-breakfast with separate cottages across Moen Bay in East Hampton. Wren will arrange activities throughout the long weekend, working in times for rehearsal and dinner, bachelor and bachelorette parties, the ceremony and reception, and brunch the next day. It's going to be an extravaganza!

"What about your gown? You put together such a beautiful selection for me to choose from. I'm not sure I can help as much with yours!" Maya giggles as her topaz eyes glitter.

"Mine too," Wren adds. "The plunging V neckline accentuated my boobs so well, I had to keep Tag from ripping it off and ruining it!"

Our laughter fills my office as Wren ducks and dodges Tag's phantom hands.

"You guys are too sweet," I say, then look at my mother. "Mom, I'd love if you would fly up and help me find a dress. I'll book appointments with my favorite designers, and we can spend a week together. Plus, you can get to know Revna and Estrid since you're already friends with Idonea."

"Oh, my little girl. My last pup to celebrate her mating. Of course! Let me know the date, and I'll hop on our jet."

"Hooray!" I exclaim and wink at the others. "The rest of you will be surprised."

My girls tease me while my mothers-in-law smile.

"Next your mates will go all Alpha male and tell you how they're 'going to put my pup in your belly.' Just like Dylan did when I went into heat," Sasha says, shaking her head.

"Exactly!" Sage and Vera agree in unison.

"Well, Rust had to convince me since I was not interested in pups at all," Natalie says, then smiles. "But I am so very thankful for our son!"

As they go on about pups, I wonder when I'll go into heat. Ordinarily, being around her mate, a she-wolf will go into heat. But I'm not surprised I haven't yet since we haven't had enough time together.

But do I want pups now? I still have to launch Signy's Secret Cache—my luxury online boutique. The trip to New York Fashion Week and the subsequent private jet crash set off a chain of events. I finally have the mindset to accomplish my goal.

One step at a time, Signy.

I set aside thoughts of pups and boutiques. No rush on either. Besides, I doubt Garrett, Dolph, and Colin are ready for little ones running around. They thoroughly enjoy the fucking part. Dirty diapers? Uh, not so much.

CHAPTER 9

arrett

"I KNOW we're about to meet with Thyra before the Ruling Council. But the thought of pups reminds me I have the urge to put my pup in Signy's belly. My wolf demands it."

"You too?"

I scrub a hand over my face as I listen to Dolph and Colin. I have to admit, I agree. Hell, my balls grow heavy with seed just thinking about it.

"Yeah, I know what you mean," I say. "Perhaps it's longevity? I'll be honest. I hadn't thought about it before that night. My focus was on pleasuring our mate. Making her cum until she begged for mercy or passed out."

Colin nods.

"Not too long ago I was anti-Signy. Now, I want Preggy Signy."

We chuckle and rib him for being such a dumbass.

"What's so funny?"

We glance towards the door at Thyra's voice. She arches an eyebrow as her eyes flick from one of us to the other.

"Care to share?"

"Uh, not really," I say and gesture towards the conference room table. "Tell us what you've got."

Her eyes lower as her checks flush. She hesitates at the door.

"I—I'm so sorry I didn't give you good intel last—"

"Nope!"

"Stop right there."

"Say no more, Thyra."

She peeks at us but shakes her head.

"I feel responsible for so many getting hurt or…"

I stride over to my younger sister and wrap her in my arms like I did when she was a pup and stubbed her toe running through the woods. She hooks an arm around my waist and buries her face in my chest. Her body trembles as she cries.

I will not allow Thyra to blame herself. She gave us the info she decoded. In no way is she responsible. I should have done better recognizance upon arrival. The fault lies with me as Alpha and as commander.

I tell her so and guide her to the table where Dolph and Colin embrace her and tell her the same.

"All right. All right. No need to get carried away, you

know," she protests as she pushes out of their arms and places her laptop on the table. "I get it, now, thanks. So, let's get down to it, shall we?"

If the situation wasn't so dire, I'd laugh at her abrupt about-face. Instead, I nod and settle in the leather chair beside her.

"Tell us what you got, especially about the missing females. We have to find them. Return the she-wolves to their packs and find packs to adopt the turned human females. They can't go back to their human way of life. We'll need to explain the situation to them. Plus, the pups. If theirs, then they stay with their mothers. If not, we find them new homes, too. First, we get them. All of them."

"The rings are more cautious now. It took a minute to figure the who, what, where..."

Thyra provides us with detailed transcripts, timelines, last-known locations, and more. She's meticulous in her findings and shares the information thoroughly, more than she has in the past.

It riles me she has any doubt in her tech abilities now. She's a wiz and a hacker I trust with all my post Green Beret missions. I make a mental note to praise her, but not so much she becomes prickly. There's a fine line with my fiery little sister.

"Apparently, the rings are ready to 'unload cargo' before they go further underground. I ordered the auction dates chronologically. The next one is in two days," she says, then shifts her gaze from the wall monitor to mine. I notice a flicker of worry in her eyes before she continues. "What will you do, Garrett?"

Even after all our missions to end these breeder rings, their heinous acts and disregard for the lives of others riles me. My hands fist as my wolf growls, fangs bared.

"We have to end these fuckers once and for all!" I shout, jumping to my feet and stalking to the window.

I stare out, not seeing the Atlantic Ocean stretching for miles. Rather, the faces of the countless frightened and abused she-wolves and turned human females float across my vision. The last image is of Signy when we rescued her. Worn and barely clothed, tears filled her eyes at seeing us.

We saved many. But not enough.

No way can we leave these rings to go hide deeper in their dark world, crawling out to destroy more lives.

"Enough!"

I pivot and lock eyes with Dolph and Colin.

"We meet with the Ruling Council. Tell them the latest and call for them to join us. You in?"

"This shit stops now."

"Finish the fuckers."

They snarl as their eyes flash with their wolves.

"I want to go."

My head snaps to Thyra. She straightens in her chair and lifts her chin. Defiant eyes bore into mine.

"I can monitor activity firsthand. Warn yo—"

"Absolutely not," I interrupt and hold a hand up to stop her protest. "I will not risk your safety. At. All. You will do as always and monitor us from here. Let go of what happened that night. It is not your fault. You are a valuable part of our team. Do you understand?"

Thyra averts her eyes and gnaws on her bottom lip.

I give her a moment to fight her inner battle to obey her Alpha or to argue.

"Yes. But"—my cocked eyebrow gives her pause, but she hurries on—"I mean, I want revenge and don't want to disappoint you again."

She ends on a whisper.

"Listen carefully, Thyra. We will get our revenge. Trust and believe. You could never disappoint. But if you mention any more about messing up that night, I will have Dolph, as beta, put you over his knee and spank you until you get over it. You are not above being punished like any other unmated she-wolf in this pack. Do you understand?"

Her jaw drops as her eyes widen. Eyebrows reach her hairline. I continue to pin her with an Alpha stare until she stutters her acceptance.

"Now, we move on."

I stride back to the table and start the video conference call. One by one, pack Alphas appear on the flat-screen television. Aspen Wolves Pack Alpha Leif Karlsson sits forward. His bottle green eyes scan the other faces.

"We're missing Jagger," he says as a square with Jagger's name pops up. "Good. Let's get this meeting started. I need to find my sister. Now."

The Las Vegas and the Sedona Alphas express the need to find their missing daughters. The others agree.

Jagger appears with Sage seated beside him. He too checks for those in attendance, then nods.

"With all present, Garrett, give us the latest," he says.

"Thyra can best speak to it," I respond and turn to her.

She doesn't hesitate to recount her findings, ending with the next auction date. She turns to me and waits.

"Thank you, Thyra. Your intel is invaluable."

The corners of her mouth lift slightly as she returns my nod.

"Alphas, if I may speak."

My gaze shifts to Sage, who sits forward. All murmur their assent.

"I recommend taking out the rings now. No need to wait for the auction. Thyra located their bases. Each one falls within a pack's territory, excluding Miami and New York. Four pairs made of the Alpha and a local witch—"

The Alphas raise their voices. But Jagger growls and glares at the camera, eyes flashing silver with his wolf close to the surface.

"You *will* respect my fated mate. She *will* finish her recommendation uninterrupted. *Then*, you may speak. Understood?"

They grumble their acknowledgment, and Sage continues, unbothered but the outburst.

"The pack's enforcers will be near on standby, awaiting communication from the Alpha. Each pair will converge on the locations simultaneously, not allowing the rings time to communicate with each other. The witch will use magick to erect a dome to contain the area, block signals, and render the ring members unconscious. The Alpha will alert the enforcers who will join them. They will apprehend the ring members, keeping the leaders alive to question. The witch will tend to the females and stay with the pack to heal them. No need to risk injuries and death to the Alphas and enforcers. Work together and get this finished."

"Hell, I'm not an Alpha. But I damn sure agree with Luna Sage," Thyra says into the silence as she shrugs her shoulders, hands raised with palms upward. "That's what I'm talking about."

"No, little wolf, you are not an Alpha," Leif grumbles. "Luna Sage, no disrespect, and we are indebted to you and your witches for helping us that night. However, wolf shifters can handle our own battles."

"I disagree, Leif," the Alpha from Las Vegas says. "My need to find my daughter ranks higher than my ego. Luna Sage suggests a fast and less risky way to end these rings and rescue the females. I vote yes and to leave as soon as the teams assemble."

"Yes! Waste no more time," the Sedona Alpha—whose daughter is also missing—says emphatically.

I add my yes vote as do the others. We wait for Leif.

"Fine. Yes," he says. "My enforcers and I are ready."

"Excellent. The witches are awaiting my call," Sage says as she brings her mobile to her ear.

"And what about New York and Miami? Do the rest of you need additional enforcers?" I ask, not wanting to be left out of the war our missions led up to.

Dolph and Colin nod.

The scent of the forest after a spring rain, woody and earthy, with a hint of wild honey straight from the comb wafts in from behind me. I turn to find Signy standing in the doorway. Her face ashen. Tears brim her eyes.

"I prefer you stay here," she whispers.

Immediately, the three of us race to her side. Hands stroke her arms and back and cup her cheeks as we move her into the hallway. So engrossed in the meeting, we missed hearing and detecting her scent. I expected to break the news to her later. But now...

"Baby, the plan Sage has is sound. Not risky with the witches using their magick to secure the rings."

Signy shakes her head. Long, silky strands sway vigorously.

"I don't care, Garrett! Not again!" She exclaims and grips my forearms, shaking them. "The witches can handle it with the Alphas. You don't need to go. *Please!*"

Signy's cry undoes me.

I lift her from her feet and crush her to my chest, vibrating with my rumble to soothe her. I hate myself for upsetting her again. Especially after telling her not to worry and to focus on our mate bonding ceremony.

She whimpers, and I rock her, burying my face in her hair.

"It's okay, baby," Dolph says gruffly, his voice thick with emotion. "Please don't cry."

Colin grips the back of her neck and tilts her face towards him.

"Oh, Little Wolf, be a good girl for us," he says before he

licks a trail of tears from her cheek. "No more tears from you."

"D—Don't leave me, then," she stutters.

"Naughty Wolf. Telling your Doms what to do," he growls and smacks her ass. "We will punish you later."

She yelps and tightens her arms around my waist, hips bucking.

I ignore my awakened cock and set her on her feet, holding her steady as she wobbles.

"We have to get back to the meeting. I can't promise we'll stay. We have to join them if needed. Now, go wait for us at home."

I spin her around and spank her ass to move her along.

She rises on her toes and pouts at me over her shoulder. I cock an eyebrow, and she rushes away. We watch until she enters the elevator at the end of the hallway, then glance at one another before we return to my office.

Thyra raises an eyebrow.

I shake my head and tune back in to the conversation.

We spend the next thirty minutes organizing the teams. As expected, the packs don't need reinforcements from New York or from Miami. We're disappointed but will standby should the need arise.

Thyra happily coordinates with the packs' tech people. Fingers fly across her keyboard as she nods and talks to them over a separate video conference call.

The meeting ends, and Dolph, Colin, and I head out to take care of our wayward mate.

igny

"You do not know how glad I am to relax finally! This past month has been beyond hectic. Teleporting from one pack to the other, making sure the females are healing and are as comfortable as expected. *Chile!*"

"Thank the gods for your ceremony weekend, Signy. Everyone needs a distraction."

I grin like the Cheshire Cat as I listen to Sage and Lillie during our ride to Manhattan in one of the pack's Sikorsky S-92 Executive Helicopters. It's day two, and the morning of my bachelorette day with my girls.

My heart is so full of love and happiness, it vibrates. My bonds with Garrett, Dolph, and Colin hum both ways with their excitement as strong as mine. At last, we can put the breeder rings behind us.

Sage's plan worked as expected. The only downside is a few turned humans who are distraught after not being allowed to return home. Having been human before mating Viggo and Tag, Maya and Wren spent time with those females. They explained the dangers to wolf shifters and to the females should humans learn of our existence. The idea of being experimented on or killed changed their minds. It'll be some time before they come to fully accept their situations.

However, a few male wolf shifters claim to sense a mate bond with some of them. But the Alphas refuse to let them act upon their attraction to allow the females to adjust. The males understand, considering the horrific ordeal the females faced.

But we'll see how long that lasts. The draw to a mate is powerful, and a male can only deny nature for so long before succumbing to madness. It's best left with the gods. They know best for all.

"And it's nice to be away from Moen Island. It's been forever since Randel let me come into the city. All the missions Alpha did made Randel super overprotective, especially since we learned a ring kidnapped Estrid while she was in the city alone all those years ago."

Vera's words pull me from my thoughts. I nod in agreement.

Thank the gods I ended up kidnapped by Blaise, who had Estrid. Otherwise, Colin may never have learned the cause of his mother leaving. All along, he and Brandt assumed she abandoned them, causing so much pain and anger.

At least some good came from those monsters.

Wren claps her hands to get everyone's attention.

"Well, boy, oh boy, do I have the best plans for Signy's Bachelorette Day! So, let's only focus on good feeling thoughts," she says.

"Do share!" I exclaim since she refuses to tell me.

Not wanting me to know what to expect for the day, Wren packed my bag and put a lock on it. So, I have zero clue.

"Now, didn't we have this conversation before, Signy?" She asks, wagging a perfectly manicured finger at me. "It's a day full of surprises you'll enjoy. Trust me."

"Fine," I grumble, then squeal.

"No pouting either, chica," Maya says as she reaches from her seat to tickle me. "Only laughter."

I give in and let all negative thoughts wash away like the waves of the Atlantic Ocean beneath the helicopter.

Fifteen minutes later, we land at the East 34th Street Heliport. Soon we disembark and head to Mercedes-Benz Sprinters driven by pack enforcers. They place our luggage in the back as we split up and climb inside each vehicle. The enforcers get in and take off. Apparently, they know where we're going.

Between chatting, I glimpse out the windows and up through the panoramic sunroof.

There's no place like New York. From the easily recognizable Manhattan skyline to the iconic yellow cabs and the bustling sidewalks where tourists and Native New Yorkers brush past one another in their own worlds. The energy is palpable, even through the Sprinter's exterior.

"Well, I'm glad you picked the city for my day, Wren. I love it, thank you!"

She grins and shimmies in her seat.

After a while, the Sprinter stops. I peek out the window for a clue while the door opens.

"Good morning, ladies. Welcome to The Mark Hotel."

"Thank you."

"*Gracias.*"

"Enjoy your stay," the smartly dressed doorman enthuses as he helps the girls from the Sprinter.

My grin widens as I step onto the sidewalk. Slowly, I spin to take in my surroundings.

"This is the most luxurious and elegant boutique hotel in Manhattan. Perfect for the Miami Pack Princess turned New York Pack Queen," Wren says as she loops her arm through mine and saunters towards the entrance. "Perfectly located on Madison Avenue overlooking Central Park. It's the ideal spot for our plans."

Two bellmen swiftly appear to take our luggage and to usher us across the black marble with an inlaid white logo that replaces the gray sidewalk. Another doorman greets us with a flourish.

"Good morning, ladies. Welcome to The Mark Hotel."

We thank him as we follow the others inside, where the concierge greets us. As she leads us to elevators, she points out the shops, lounges, and restaurants. Once we exit the elevator on the sixteenth floor, she opens glossy black double doors and steps back for us to enter. We enter a sun-filled reception foyer with a gorgeous floral arrangement on the table.

"Welcome to the Penthouse Suite," she says as she joins us. "It's the largest in the United States, over two full floors, plus a private rooftop terrace…"

She continues the tour of the lavish space decorated in a soft palette of white, cream, beige, brown, and gray. Natural light from the many windows and skylights floods the rooms. An expansive living room with a twenty-six-foot ceiling, a dining room for ten and a kitchenette, a library, five bedrooms with en suite bathrooms, powder rooms, a conservatory leading upstairs to a second library, a roof pavilion, and the terrace spanning the roof.

I gasp as much at the commanding view across Central Park and the skyline as from the gorgeous table set for a scrumptious breakfast with servers at the ready. I rush over to Wren and hug her.

"Oh! This is spectacular! If this is the start of our day, I can only imagine what the rest will be."

She squeezes me back and nods.

"Oh, honey, you ain't seen nothing yet! Now, let's eat."

As we end the delicious meal, Wren tells everyone to change into outfit number one. She comes with me to the primary bedroom suite, where the maid arranged my clothing in one of two walk-in closets. Dresses I've never seen before hang on silk hangers with numbers on them.

She selects a red, black, and white mini dress I recognize as a classic PUCCI print on hanger number one and picks up a pair of gold sandals with long, thin ankle straps. She tucks a red handbag under her arm and grins at me.

"Outfit number one ready for you," she says, striding to the dressing area. "You get ready while I go change. We'll meet in the living room."

"Nice choice, Wren! You know they're one of my favorite designers."

She winks and leaves, wiggling her fingers over her shoulder.

Moments later, we're in front of the hotel. Each of us wears cute dresses and heels.

"Okay, Sig. Next up, you're favorite pastime—"

"Shopping!" The girls chorus, clapping their hands.

I giggle and shimmy my hips.

We visit all my favorite boutiques along Madison Avenue until we end up on Fifty-seventh Street and Fifth Avenue at Bergdorf Goodman. The venerated retail mecca of class, elegance, and sophistication for women, men, children, and home has it all.

Once we leave Bergdorf's we head south to Saks Fifth Avenue where we have lunch at L'Avenue At Saks. Once again, the New York City skyline dazzles us from the terraces as we eat delectable French food and sip Champagne.

Afterwards, we take a leisurely stroll along Park Avenue, heading north to The Mark on Seventy-seventh Street. The fragrance of blossoming flowers wafts over from the medians. I tilt my head back, eyes closed, to inhale deeply as the sun shines on my face. I couldn't be happier with my special day.

"Oh Wren, this is amazing. It's been too long since I enjoyed myself with my girls. I'm so glad all of you came," I say, glancing at each of them.

"We could never miss your ceremony, Signy. And be sure we'll visit regularly. I love Miami. But New York is something else!" Natalie says.

"And don't forget, Dylan and I split our time between here and Miami. We're right over on Fifty-seventh Street, near to Bergdorf's," Sasha adds.

I give her a hug, and we continue.

When we enter the penthouse suite, Wren corrals us away from the living room, insisting we go to our rooms and change into outfit number two. She gives us twenty minutes to meet in the living room.

I'm surprised to find a hot pink PVC scallop-edged playsuit with crossover halter neck bra, belt, and matching collar attached to the thong by a strip. A pair of fuck-me stilettos completes the look. I grin as I head to the shower imagining my mates' faces if they saw me in the sexy as sin lingerie. Then wonder what the heck Wren has planned.

As I leave my bedroom suite, my enhanced hearing picks up the sound of music filtering from the living room. I hurry my pace to find out what's happening. At the entryway, I slap a hand over my mouth.

The staff transformed the room into a posh burlesque club. The canopy of an opulent ruby velvet tent hides the soaring ceiling. A crystal chandelier hangs from the peak, flashing prisms on the ruby silk sides of the tent. Dozens of oversized pillows cover the floor of suede squares in shades of ruby. A fully stocked bar stands to one side. My mouth drops at the sight of two stripper poles reaching through the canopy, giant champagne glasses, and ballet barres.

A DJ—barefoot and dressed in a black half-face mask, suspenders, and pants—spins sensuous music piped in from hidden speakers strategically placed to heighten the hedonistic vibe. It thrums erotically.

"You must be the bride-to-be."

A petite bombshell emerges from behind the open flap. The corset, suspenders, and G-string accentuate her ample curves. Her crimson lips widen in a smile.

"I'm Scarlet, your instructor," she says, extending her hand then gesturing behind her. "And this is my squad."

"Surprise!"

I jump at the cries of my girls from behind me. They rush over dressed in similar sexy lingerie. A bartender—styled like the DJ—offers us a silver tray with signature pink cocktails. We raise them for a toast.

"Let Part II of Signy's Bachelorette Day begin!" Wren says.

Scarlet and her squad move to the apparatuses and begin their routines. We watch, mesmerized by their agility and grace. No sooner do I finish my drink than Scarlet takes my hand and leads me to the poles. She shows me some moves, then steps back for me to try.

"That's it, Signy! Use your inner thigh muscles. Squeeze like it's Garrett between them!"

"Yeah, baby! Show 'em what you got, girl!"

"Chica! Look at you!"

I grin at my girls as I hang upside down, gripping the stripper pole between my legs. No male strippers. But a few female ones and burlesque dancers make my bachelorette party a blast!

It was Maya's idea—Ms. Fitness. She took burlesque dance classes to change up her program and fell in love with them. She asked Scarlet, a world-famous Las Vegas burlesque performer, to do my party. They flew her and some of her dancer friends over to teach us.

Wren arranged for a videographer and a photographer —both female—to capture the happenings and will give each of us a video and an album as keepsakes.

"OMG! My boob!" I laugh as my breast slips from the halter top bra.

I'm not concerned the guys see anything since Wren made sure to hire men who prefer to ogle men and not my tits. So, I don't let the mishap stop my show.

When Scarlet tells me to round up and grasp as high up the pole as possible, I just do it. Better than Nike any day! Once upright, I pull my bra back in place, kick out my legs parallel to the floor, and throw my head back with a whoop. Gracefully, I drop to a squat and bow my head.

The girls stomp and clap while the DJ hypes me up over the mic.

I hug Scarlet, and she tells me how well I perform. She

even says I can make a guest appearance at her show in Vegas whenever I'm in Sin City. I don't hesitate to accept her invitation, knowing my mates would get a kick out of it as long as I wear a mask and a wig. Well… maybe. But it would be loads of fun if the Las Vegas Pack Alpha grants us permission to enter his territory.

With stars in my eyes, I give the stage to Natalie. She hops up and does a few stretches they showed us earlier to limber up. Her eyes shine bright with enthusiasm as she tightens her high ponytail.

We applaud when she grabs the pole and swings herself up onto it.

The bartender comes around with another tray of cocktails. We snag glasses and root Natalie on. I do a wolf whistle with my fingers in my mouth—a trick I learned as a kid from Viggo.

"Go on, Willow! It's your turn!"

"Yeah, Willow!"

She takes the challenge and leaps onto the stage.

"I'm ready to outdo all of you!" She boasts good-naturedly.

We whistle and whoop to encourage her performance. And she dazzles us with an upside-down split. When she finishes her routine, she throws her arms up in victory.

The instructors place crystal embellished crowns on our heads. Mine has bride written on it in pink stones. I laugh and hug each of my girls as I thank them for making my day so special and unforgettable.

"Oh, but it's not over yet!" Wren says. "Moving on to

Part III. Ladies, you know what to do. Outfit three awaits. Meet in the library in ten minutes."

I return to my suite to find a pair of baby pink silk pajamas with pink marabou mules in the dressing room. After a quick shower, I slip into the pj's and mules, then join the others. Once again, the staff transformed a room. This time a home theater replaces the bookshelves and furniture. Comfy leather chaise lounges face a projector screen. A concessions display with a popcorn maker and more pink cocktails stands in the back corner. The bartender swapped his mask for an apron and passes us candies and tubs of buttery popcorn.

"So, what's the movie?" I ask as I plop down next to Sasha.

"In keeping with the burlesque theme… first up… *Striptease*," Wren announces.

Everyone claps and settles in.

We watch movies, eat popcorn, and drink until after midnight.

As we part for our suites, Wren holds up a hand.

"We'll end Signy's Bachelorette Day with breakfast on the terrace before we fly back to Moen Island. Outfit number four. Sweetest of dreams."

Being the bride, I don't share while the others pair up.

My mobile rings as I place it on the nightstand. I smile when I recognize Dolph's ringtone and accept the call.

"Good night, baby."

"We'll see you tomorrow."

"We love you."

"Good night, my loves. I love you more," I whisper past a yawn before I end the call.

My eyelids droop closed as dreams of my fairytale wedding play in my mind. The corners of my mouth tilt up as I sigh contented. The start of our happily ever after comes with the dawn.

olin

"WELL, my friends, this time tomorrow you'll be happily mated males and join the likes of Tag, Dylan, Rust, Viggo, and me in the bliss of eternal union. Here's to you and your beautiful bride-to-be!"

Jagger raises his crystal snifter in a toast.

The glint of prisms reminds me of Signy's twinkling eyes after I've wrung multiple orgasms from her sweet, juicy pussy, and we—

"Damn, Colin. Get a grip on yourself with that goofy ass smile on your face, Mr. I'm Too Cool to Care."

Along with Jagger and the rest of the Miami Wolves Pack, Randel, and some enforcers guffaw.

The tantalizing image of a sated Signy spread before me

dissipates as Leif's bellow and their resulting laughter resound around the room.

I heave a disappointed sigh at the loss and refocus on our bachelor party, or Bro Bonding, as Viggo calls it.

We're in the private Bullmoose Room at Keens Steakhouse in the city. The best place for male wolf shifters to eat big ass cuts of savory meat and to partake of top-shelf whiskey. It's a spot we frequent to unwind after a day at the office or to get a break from Moen Island. I rarely smoke. But this is a special occasion for fine Cuban cigars Tag brought up from Miami.

I take a long draw on one and settle back in my leather club chair. The tasting notes of the spicy, earthy, and woody flavors linger on my palate. They blend well with the smoky, dark berries flavor of the whiskey. Its trademark bite drags along the back of my tasting.

Much like my delectable and tantalizing Signy.

The thought makes my mind drift again.

The restaurant is near the West 30th Street Heliport we flew in to earlier.

Signy and her damn take on human traditions. First, no more sex until our mate bonding ceremony night. Then we couldn't see her before the ceremony, which meant no wrapping my larger frame around her lush curves in an attempt at relief for my aching balls last night…

Fuuuck.

I don't know about Garrett and Dolph. But I rubbed one out in the shower before we left the island. Tomorrow can't come soon enough. Pun intended. And I'm making it my duty to edge Signy until she begs to orgasm. Payback, Little Wolf.

"Who would've thought the mighty military men would fall so hard for a *feilan*"—Leif shakes his head and his bottle green eyes sparkle with mischief—"Dolph, sure. But Garrett and definitely not Colin... mmm mmm. A *little wolf* gotcha. Surprise!"

Everyone chuckles, knowing Dolph is the nurturer of us three, Garrett the grumpy Alpha. And me? The badass who doesn't give a fuck. Put us all together for one she-wolf? Whoa. Even I'm surprised.

I laugh harder and shake my head.

"Only the gods know what's planned," Randel says sagely.

We turn and throw roasted nuts at him. He raises his hands and ducks, laughing.

"Okay! Okay," he chuckles. "I'm know because I mated first. Trust me. I had no interest in one she-wolf, except for a night, maybe two. Then bam! Vera."

He pauses and cocks his eyebrow with a nod, then raises his glass for a toast.

"Best of luck to you. All *three* of you!" He proclaims with a smirk.

I stand and stride over to Garrett and Dolph, then gesture for them to rise. Shoulder to shoulder, we stand and raise our snifters high, knowing we will forever cherish our fated mate, the one and only love of our lives.

"Keep your luck, little brother. We have Signy," Garrett says with a matching smirk.

"Exactly!" Dolph adds.

I nod and toss back my whiskey.

"The gods are good," I say, then stride to the bar. "Last round, then we're out. I know you need your beauty sleep, Rust."

"Fuck you, Colin."

I chuckle and pour whiskey in his snifter.

Later, as we board the helicopter bound for Moen Island, Tag's mobile rings with a call from Wren to confirm the girls turned in for the night. After we settle in our seats, Dolph calls our mobiles and adds Signy. She answers with a sleepy voice, and I smile.

"Good night, baby."

"We'll see you tomorrow."

"We love you."

"Good night, my loves. I love you more," she whispers, yawning before she ends the call.

Each of us turns to stare out windows, lost in our thoughts, silent for the rest of the ride.

As I crawl into bed at my mansion, I thank the gods for my fated mate.

DOLPH

"WAKE UP. Or the early wolf will get the babe. *Again.*"

A nudge, and I jolt awake. Colin—bare chested and dressed in shorts—stands beside the bed, grinning at me.

"A workout to release this pent-up sexual frustration, lunch, then get ready for our babe," he says. "And boy, am I already ready for her!"

I sit up with a groan, willing my morning wood to go away for the last unfulfilled time. Signy's no sex rule sucks.

"Yeah. I know how you feel," Garrett says from the foot of the bed. "It's been a challenge, especially with her flitting about in mini dresses all weekend. Visions of those long legs wrapped around my hips as I pound into her naked pussy just won't stop. They're on repeat."

He grips the back of his neck and shakes his head.

I grunt in agreement and head to my en suite bathroom. When I emerge, they're in the sitting room, pacing the floor.

"Let's go," I say and stride to the double doors.

Once outside, we jog to the island's fitness center. Along the way, members of the pack wave and offer congratulations. We notice silk ribbons in shades of pink, cream, and gold wrapped around lampposts and wrought-iron posts topped with flower arrangements. Members placed floral wreaths in the ceremony colors on their mansion doors, while shops did the same. The entire island is set to celebrate.

A grin spreads across my face as I think of how busy Signy and Wren have been with the planning. Along with Sigrid, Wren practically lived on Moen Island these past couple of weeks. Sasha and Dylan stayed at their

Manhattan penthouse and flew over regularly. I'm glad Signy has her family and friends helping her and happier she's building new relationships with Thyra, Vera, and our mothers. Our Queen is setting in for good.

"Okay, Goofy Number Two."

Garrett nudges me in the ribs and continues, "I can always tell when you and Colin think about Signy."

"And what about you, Mr. Grumpy Turned to Mr. Mushy?" Colin counters. "You soften up right quick when Signy is around."

Garrett smirks.

"On the contrary. I'm diamond hard when Signy is around. Listen for her screams tonight," he says.

We continue to rib each other as we enter the fitness center. It's busy with males and she-wolves getting in morning workouts. Leif turns and waves us over to the free weights area where he lifts with Dylan and Rust.

"Ready to tie the knot the wolf's way?" He chuckles. "Your *feilan* has three to take. Gods help her!"

"When Sasha went into heat, even I got worn out," Dylan says.

For him—an MMA trained fighter—to tire during his mate's heat makes me wonder about our stamina. We're fit as hell. But I've heard stories about the male's constant need to fuck his she-wolf through the days of her heat until she's with pup.

So far, Signy has shown no signs of her heat. Who knows when or if she will.

I set the thoughts aside and grip a set of dumbbells off

the rack. At lease tonight and during our honeymoon, we'll make up for the time Signy halted our sex lives. My cock twitches in my shorts. I start some biceps curls and focus on my set. No one needs to see my giant dick punching a hole in my shorts.

After our sessions, we stretch out in the sauna and drink water before we shower. Leif joins us while Dylan returns to his mate. Leif rags him. But Dylan shrugs and jogs away.

"Your females whipped you guys," Leif chuckles. "Not for me, thanks."

"When the she-wolf meant for you appears, I'll be the first to laugh in your face," Garrett says.

We head across the road to one of the island's restaurants. My stomach growls at the aroma of steaks sizzling on the grill. Members already eating greet us with congratulations and raise their glasses. We thank them and settle at a table in the center.

"Good morning, Alpha, beta, Colin," a server says. "Everyone wishes you the best and can't wait for your ceremony."

"Thank you, Carla," Garrett says as Colin and I do the same.

"What would you like?"

We don't need to bother with a menu since they'll fix whatever we want. After the intense workout, I'm ready for a pile of steaks, raw or cooked. We order, and she heads for the kitchen.

Lunch satisfies my hunger for food. But as time moves

closer to the start of the ceremony, my hunger for Signy grows. Leif returns to the bed-and-breakfast to change. The three of us split at our mansions to get ready. My thoughts wander to Signy.

~

SIGNY

"YOU LOOK SO STUNNING, SIGNY!" Sage gushes as she touches a handkerchief under her teary eyes.

"Oh, how absolutely stunning and sexy!" Lillie exclaims.

"Simply divine," sighs Natalie.

"The guys will snatch you away before the ceremony even starts!" Laughs Vera.

I feel all that they say and more while I stand before the full-length mirror in the sitting room of our mansion's bedroom suite. Reem Acra outdid herself.

The sensuous lines hug my curves and dramatically flare into an elegant, cathedral-length mermaid train. I peer over my shoulder at the cut-out in the back that makes it as much of an exit dress as the deep-vee in the front makes a statement. The fitted long sleeves add a touch of the demure to the provocative gown. The impeccable detail of the lace exemplifies the craftsmanship of her atelier. It's a masterpiece.

The traditions continue. My mother's diamond earrings adorn my ears as something old and to have her close to me. My gown represents the new. Idonea lent Garrett's grandmother's diamond hair clips to me as the borrowed. Wren gifted me a lace G-string for the blue—perfect for fidelity.

So we don't see each other before we exchange our vows, we set our photo session for after the ceremony while guests enjoy the cocktail hour. I'm not risking a single thing.

"Signy?"

The photographer and videographer call for me to pose alone and with my nieces and nephews dressed in matching outfits, then with my mother and my mothers-in-law. They followed us discreetly throughout the day, capturing candid shots. Garrett, Dolph, and Colin have a set following them, too. We want to see all that happened while we were apart.

Wren claps her hands and tells us it's time.

My heart jumps. I hold back the tinge of panic with deep breaths. Opening my eyes, I ask for a moment of privacy, then walk to the windows and stare out towards the forest beyond. I reflect on my childhood on Moon Island in Miami and the life I had leading me to my fated mates. My eyes close, and I whisper a prayer of love and thanks.

One more deep cleansing breath, and I walk to the suite door. My father Marcus waits just outside. He scans my face with concern. I smile and air kiss his cheeks to let him know I'm all right. When I pull back, his eyes shine with tears. He takes a moment to collect himself. Then extends his arm for me to hold.

Wren hands my bouquet to me and gives me air kisses, too. She adjusts my train behind me and fluffs my veil into place. We join the others outside and slip inside the SUVs for the ride to the center of the island.

The ribbons on the lampposts guide us to the garden. Where amidst the flowers and benches stand rows of long rectangular tables with pale pink tablecloths with gold and cream place settings surrounded by gold wooden chairs. Floral arrangements line the center with buckets of Champagne. Chafing dishes with a variety of foods and beverages sit on tables to the side. A separate table holds a five-tiered cake. Columns of intertwined tree branches and flowers strung with thousands of fairy lights surround the area to allow for the celebration to continue after the sun sets. A ceremony bower with the same treatment stands at one end. I smile at the magickal fairy-tale, all thanks to Sage.

"Ready, honey?" My father asks as he extends his arm.

I take a final deep breath and smile as I place my hand on his arm.

Time to complete the mate bonding ceremony with Garrett, Dolph, and Colin. Finally.

~

Garrett

· · ·

THE PACK GATHERS in front of the bower while the three of us wait beneath it with my father. Ordinarily, I would preside over the ceremony as the pack Alpha. However, with me as a mate, Arne will do the honors. His smile widens, and I turn to find Signy at the end of the aisle.

I barely notice her nieces and nephews preceding her as they drop red rose petals on the pale pink runner. Except for Signy, Dolph, and Colin, all disappear from my view.

The music changes, and the air crackles with electricity. The guests rise.

Like a vision, Signy takes my breath away. The sunlight beams down to highlight her ethereal beauty.

Her radiant smile is more brilliant than the multitude of diamonds that adorn her ears and her hair. The stones flash as she moves forward in a gown that makes my cock harden.

She's heart-stoppingly gorgeous.

A hush comes over the guests as they marvel along with me at Signy's beauty. Her eyes flick from mine to Dolph and Colin, who flank me. Mine remains on hers as she walks down the aisle on Marcus' arm.

It takes all my well-known self-discipline to anchor my feet to the platform to prevent myself from rushing to Signy and sweeping her into my arms. I want to carry her away to our den. Colin shifts on his feet while Dolph rumbles. They share the same urge, just as I sense her excitement through our mate bond. She beams at us, and I return her smile.

Standing before us, we step forward and bring her beneath the bower. In unison, the three of us speak.

"Signy Larson, we claim you as our fated mate to protect, love, and cherish for all time. To bear our pups and to stand by our sides. We love you, Signy Moen Pihl Voll, our fated mate!"

Her throat works as she swallows back tears of joy, then clears her throat to respond.

"Garrett Moen, Dolph Pihl, Colin Voll, I claim you as my fated mates to protect, love, and cherish for all time. To bear your pups and to stand by your sides. I love you, Garrett Moen, Dolph Pihl, Colin Voll, my fated mates!"

The pack erupts in shouts and howls of celebration while the three of us take turns kissing Signy. As Colin lifts her from a dip, I raise my hands for silence.

Dolph takes her left hand as I slip a flawless oval-cut diamond on a platinum band set with round-cut diamonds and a matching eternity band on her ring finger. Her breath catches at the beauty of the sparkling gems.

Signy is no longer the Miami Pack Princess. She's the New York Pack Queen, our mate who we will shower with more than just jewels. We will give her our all.

More tears fill her eyes, and I use my thumb to swipe them away gently as the three of us murmur words of everlasting love. Once she places platinum wedding bands on our fingers, I feel complete.

Colin scoops her up and swings her around. Her head goes back as she howls with joy. We join her for a song of love. Then he carries her back up the aisle as the pack congratulates us. We settle at the head table. Once everyone takes their seats, my father stands with a flute of Champagne.

"Congratulations to you! Here's to my son, his best friends, and our new daughter!"

Cheers fill the air.

Jagger rises and raises his flute.

"Tonight, we celebrate not only their mate bonding, but the joining of the Miami and New York Wolves Packs!"

I stand, bringing Signy up with me as the space rings with the howls of dozens of wolf shifters. Dolph and Colin flank us.

"We celebrate Our Queen with a feast and a wolf run!"

As more shouts erupt, Thyra makes her way to stand before our table and lifts her flute.

"Signy, I want to—"

"*Mate!*"

Thyra jerks as though zapped by electricity. Her eyes widen, mouth forms a perfect O.

I jump to my feet, scanning the area for the source of the animalistic roar.

Crystal shatters as silverware clatters against the china. A she-wolf screams. Several males growl and rise to their feet. Enforcers step up.

My gaze shifts to spot a wild-eyed Leif charging past tables, pushing chairs and pack members aside. The wind tosses his flaming red hair as he rushes forward, eyes locked on Thyra.

"*Mine!*"

She gapes at me as a cry escapes her. She trembles but doesn't move as Leif barrels towards her.

I leap over the table and land between him and my little sister. My wolf snarls at the threat.

"What the fuck, Leif?" I growl, on the verge of shifting. My eyes flash cobalt blue as he nears. "Hold the hell up!"

I push Alpha command at him. He staggers but regains his footing and steps closer.

"My. Mate. Her."

He snaps out the words as he points behind me at Thyra. She whimpers.

A deep rumbling rises from his chest.

"Oh, *Minn Feilan*," he croons. "I don't mean to scare you, *My Little Wolf*. I couldn't source your unique scent until now. You're my fated mate."

He steps forward, and I growl.

"Hold your overprotective horses, Big Brother."

My head snaps sideways to find Thyra strutting closer. Eyebrows dipped and lips pursed. She glances up at me.

"You were just scared a second ago—"

"Yeah, well. He shocked me with some Alpha super-power. I'm fine now and can handle my own business. Thank you very much."

Now, my mouth gapes at her ability to 180, even in the face of a feral male wolf shifter.

She pats my chest and turns to Leif. He reaches for her, and she puts a hand up palm out.

"Uh-uh. The same goes for you, Big Boy. I'll hear you out. But don't get it in your head to go all possessive caveman and drag me away. Not happening with this she-wolf. You've gotta earn me."

The corners of Leif's mouth lift as his eyes gleam with emerald fire.

"Oh, you're as feisty as you are curvy, *Minn Feilan,*" he croons.

She smirks and crooks her finger. He follows her like a love-struck pup, and not a powerful Alpha.

I watch as they leave the garden, then shake my head.

"You forgot to laugh in his face."

I throw my head back and laugh at Colin's quip.

A small hand slips into mine as the scent of the forest after a spring rain, woody and earthy, with a hint of wild honey straight from the comb surrounds me.

I glance down at my fated mate and smile.

"If I can handle three growly males, Thyra can handle one," she says giggling, then tugs my hand. "Dance with me, my love."

Like a love-struck pup, I pull her into my arms. I press my lips to the shell of her ear.

"But know this, I am a possessive caveman, and once we are on our honeymoon, you will not get away from me."

She trembles.

I chuckle wickedly, looking forward to fulfilling my vow.

CHAPTER 12

igny

"This has to be the most superb boat I've ever been on. And that's saying something since we have *Moonbeam*, a fabulous 465-foot megayacht. I think it's the James Bond effect with those three tall as all heck carbon-fiber masts. I mean, they're ginormous! Just look at them."

My eyes pop as I gape at *Blue Moon*. Their mega sailing yacht may only have four feet on the Miami Wolves Pack's *Moonbeam*. But it's the design by a renowned architect and the addition of the masts to the motor that win the prize for *Blue Moon*. The tour they gave me shows an interior as incredible as the exterior.

Designed to slice through the waves, its sleek silver hull's arrow-sharp bow widens to four wedding cake tier decks in the stern. Keeping with the aerodynamic design, the sides remain smooth until hidden doors drop open to reveal various sized decks. They're perfect for sunbathing on chaise lounges or for diving off into the Atlantic Ocean, where one can play with the water toys.

That is unless one prefers to swim in the full-size pool on the second deck beneath the retractable floor of the top deck. Or perhaps the many entertainment salons fit one's fancy for games, bowling, theater-style movies. Or when one wants to work out in the fitness center, then relax in the sauna before being pampered in the spa.

Enjoy delicious meals in the dining salon or on the dining deck beneath the stars, followed by digestifs in one of the grand salons. Then end the night in the primary cabin while as many as eighteen guests slumber in the other nine oversized cabin suites.

Naturally, *Blue Moon* requires a crew of fifty-four to navigate the waters and to care for one's every whim. And it's to the crew consisting of New York Wolves Pack members Garrett introduced me to when we boarded *Blue Moon* from the tender.

After our next-day brunch with the ceremony guests, he, Dolph, and Colin surprised me with a flight down to The Bahamas where *Blue Moon* docks during the winters. We'll spend our honeymoon leisurely sailing back up to Moen Island.

"We're glad you like *Blue Moon* and sailing for our honeymoon. We figure you're a Miami girl who loves the water and would enjoy it aboard our pack's boat," Dolph says.

The sunlight glints off his aviator sunglasses and creates a halo around his buzzed golden hair as we stand at the bow. The warm breeze carries his musky masculine scent to wrap around me. My nipples pucker beneath my maxi dress as my pussy clenches. The memory of last night fills my mind. Unconsciously, I rub my ass.

"You teased us all weekend sashaying around in mini dresses showing off those long ass legs of yours. Then you change from your wedding dress into another mini dress and danced around waving your arms overhead, raising the hem."

"Now, we show you what happens to naughty little she-wolves..."

They spanked and edged me until I begged them to fuck me hard. My pussy soaks my thong as I remember their dominance and savagery. Two weeks of that, on this?

"Oh, I'm most definitely glad, and we'll enjoy *Blue Moon's* every. Single. Inch."

Clit-tingling growls rise before Colin lunges forward, tosses me over his shoulder, and marches off. I giggle, then squeal when his hand connects with my ass. He cups the spot, keeping the sting burning until I moan and circle my hips.

"Still naughty, we see," Garrett says.

Heat spreads in my lower belly at his smokey voice. I mewl, lifting trying to see his handsome face. My hooded gaze reaches his chest.

"You want to see me, naughty little wolf?" He asks as his

hand grips my throat like a collar. His face comes into view as he lifts my torso higher. "Here I am."

He claims my mouth in a searing kiss. With hungry growls, he swallows my moans.

I reach for his chest, needing to feel him. My fingers grapple at his T-shirt, bunching the soft cotton in my hands. The solid pecs beneath it flex. He groans as my fingertips brush his nipple.

"Damn, Garrett. Let Colin get her to the cabin already. Selfish bastard."

I whimper as Dolph pulls on Garrett's shoulder. He growls at the separation but doesn't resist. It's amazing how easily they share me. No testosterone-fueled fighting for control, despite being Alpha males. Yet, I love how each one wants me desperately and can't wait to join in.

I sag over Colin's back, catching my breath from the kiss.

He ignores the elevator and bounds up the staircase. My hands tighten on his waist as I jostle on his shoulder.

"Careful with her!" Dolph calls out. "And you better not drop her."

"Like I don't know that," Colin retorts.

We enter the primary cabin, where he tosses me to the center of the giant bed.

I bounce amongst the midnight blue silk pillows. Long strands of my hair cover my face, and I swipe them behind my ears. My eyes meet three ravenous gazes. My skin sizzles as red-hot sparks zip across my body. A frisson of erotic energy teases my clit, bringing forth more wetness from my throbbing pussy.

"I need you, my fated mates," I purr as my arms stretch towards them and my thighs splay open. "It's been too long."

"Your mile-high fucking for over two hours wasn't enough for you?" Garrett growls as he grips the back of his T-shirt and rips it over his head.

The tip of my tongue darts out to lick my lips in a slow circle as I stare at his sculpted torso. Tattoos ripple as his muscles flex.

Movement to my left draws my attention to Colin. Slowly, he lifts the hem of his black T-shirt. Inch by inch, chiseled abs emerge. But it's the feathery trail of tawny hair dipping below his low-slung black sweatpants that commands my attention. My mouth waters at the massive bulge the trail leads to.

"You're drooling, Little Wolf," he says with a throaty chuckle. "But don't worry. I'll lick all your juices."

My knees snap together as my thighs rub, seeking relief for my needy core. A moan slips past my parted lips.

"Oh, no, Naughty Girl," Dolph tsks. "You do not pleasure yourself unless we give you permission."

"And we have not," Garrett chides with a cocked eyebrow. "So, what does that mean?"

My cheeks flush. I lower my gaze and swallow.

"You'll punish me?"

Even as I ask, my pulse quickens and my pussy gushes, knowing the answer. Who knew I'm a pain slut?

All three tilt their heads back and sniff the air. They groan in unison as my musky arousal filters through their noses. Their eyes lower to pin me with fierce, possessive, sensual expressions.

I stare back with half-mast eyes as I rise to my knees and untie the halter string of my maxi dress. The front drops to reveal my heavy breasts tipped with pebbled nipples. I cup them and tug at the distended tips, then glide my hands down the flat plane of my belly to shimmy out of the maxi dress. My tits bounce with the movement of my hips and as I toss the dress off the bed.

My eyes remain on them until I lower into the humble submissive punishment position. Shins on the bed, knees bent wide apart, ass high, back long, forehead on the bed bracketed by forearms crossed at the wrist, and fingers flat. My waist-length hair drapes over one arm to the bed.

"My apologies, Sirs," I whisper huskily.

"Fuck. Me."

"Damn."

"Well, shit."

I bite my lower lip to hold back a giggle. I may be a sub. But I hold power over my Doms.

They descend on me for an ocean-deep fucking.

DOLPH

. . .

"Is your regulator on properly?" I ask Signy as we stand on the beach club deck at the stern of *Blue Moon*. I scan her from head to toe to ensure she's kitted out for scuba diving. "How about your tank? It's not too much on your shoulders?"

Her eyes dance behind the mask as she nods and gives me a thumbs-up.

"Normally, I'd tell Dolph to lay off with the 21 questions. But we can't have you diving half-cocked, babe," Colin says as he circles around her, eyeing every inch of the gear.

"I agree," Garrett adds as he zips her wetsuit all the way up.

She pops the regulator from her mouth and purses her lips.

"Guys. This is not my first time diving. I've been PADI Advanced Ocean Water Diver certified for years," she says, then grins. "I could probably teach you a thing or two."

Colin snorts.

"Green Berets, baby. Not much you can teach us," he says and lifts her regulator to her mouth. "Now, open up, mouthy girl. It's either this or this."

He swivels his hips and nudges her groin with his.

I chuckle and put my regulator in my mouth, then flip-flop my way to the edge of the platform. The others join me. Garrett and Colin drop in while I wait for Signy to go. She gives a little wave and follows them. I step off after she surfaces near them.

We spend the next forty-five minutes diving a wreck

off The Bahamas. The ocean turned it into an underwater paradise. The crystal-clear water offers visibility for miles, allowing us to watch colorful fish swim in and around the reef. We explore the sunken ship before we resurface.

The deckhands help us climb back on board and take our gear. They avert their gazes as Signy unzips her wetsuit to reveal a tiny white bikini. We watch as she slides the wetsuit over her shoulders, then down her legs. Bent over, her tits jiggle as she frees her feet.

"That was so much—"

She trails off as she sees us staring.

"You're as bad as horny teenagers," she giggles and thanks the female deckhand, who offers a towel. "I mean really!"

The female deckhand ducks her head to hide a smile as she passes towels to us.

"Can't help it if you act like Halle Berry as Jinx. You're our Bond Girl," Colin snickers.

"Well, then, I'll have to get an orange bikini like hers and a white belt with a silver S," Signy says, eyes twinkling. "Oh, and be a sexy badass spy!"

"Best believe you're already sexy as fuck," I say, grabbing her hips and pulling her flush to my body.

She laughs and wraps her arms around my neck.

"Thank you, my love," she says. "Or shall I call you, Pihl. Dolph Pihl?"

"You can call me whatever you want," I murmur against her lips, then kiss her breathless.

"If this lip-lock action keeps going, you can forget about jet skiing to that private beach," Colin says.

Signy breaks our kiss.

"Oh, no! I want to see it. You promised," she pouts.

I give her a last squeeze, then let her go.

"The chief steward organized the lunch. They already brought the food over on the tender, Alpha," a deckhand says.

Garrett looks to Signy, who clasps her hands and widens her eyes.

"Whatever your Luna wants," he says with a grin.

She claps her hands and bounces over to jump on him. He cups her ass as she wraps her legs around his waist and peppers his face with kisses. We join in with his laughter.

"Keep this up, and we won't make it to the beach after all," I say with a smirk.

Once again, Signy stops and turns to the deckhand.

"We're ready!"

The deckhand radios to request the jet skis from the water toy garage accessible via a hidden side panel. Minutes later, deckhands ride four jet skis to the beach club deck. We swap places and take off for the private beach.

"Eat my wake!" Signy yells as she revs the engine.

"Oh, I'll eat more than that!" I yell after her.

Garrett and Colin's laughter trails behind them as they race to catch her.

We zip through the waves, bouncing over each other's wakes. Colin shows off with figure-eights while Garrett stays close to Signy. As we near the island, she slows and points, then flashes a brilliant smile at us.

"Gorgeous!" She exclaims.

A gentle breeze blows the white gauzy canopy with its four posts covered in ropes of yellow elder The Bahamas' national flower and the purple flowers from their tree of life. The canopy floats above a table set for four with a floral bouquet at its center. Chairs have more gauzy material draped over them with a bow in the back and a wreath of flowers. The billowy topper resembles the clouds above and the table appears as one of the many islands of the country.

Bamboo torches around the perimeter and white tapers on the table will provide lighting once the sun sets below the line of the cliffs.

We'll move to the sunbed covered in white, sumptuous bedding beneath a second gauzy canopy. A bonfire to the side and more bamboo torches situated nearby, ready to be lit. Next to the sunbed, bottles of Signy's favorite rosé Champagne and four flutes chill in a bucket nestled in the sand. We'll make love to her beneath the stars.

A romantic evening I coordinated with the chief steward. So, call me the nurturer. I take care of my mate.

We bring the jet skis to the surf, and I lift Signy off hers into a bridal carry.

Speechless, she drapes an arm over my neck as she continues to stare at the setting. Her gaze darts from the table to the servers and the sunbed.

As we near the table, the tropical scent of the flowers

mingles with the aromas from the tantalizing dishes on the white linen tabletop.

I nuzzle her neck and inhale her alluring scent. Combined with her natural musk, it surpasses any of the tropical flowers and foods that surround us.

"Oh, Dolph," she breathes at last as I set her on a chair. She cups my face and continues. "I don't know what to say. You treat me so well—"

Her words catch in her throat. She glances away with tears shimmering in her eyes as her hands drop to her lap.

I crouch beside her and lift them to my lips. I place a kiss on the tip of each finger and on her palms.

Her eyes remain averted as she shakes her head.

The situation overcomes her, I muse. However, I will not allow her to sit quietly.

"Signy, you fill our hearts like no other female. We never expected to find our fated mate. But we did, and you please us beyond our wildest dreams. We only want to please you each and every second, baby."

The words pour from my heart unchecked.

The breath I didn't realize I was holding falls from my lips when Signy lifts her tear-filled eyes to gaze at me. Her chin wobbles as she sucks in a breath.

I stroke my thumb over her bottom lip before I cover it in an emotion-filled kiss. I pour my heart and soul into it. My body backs up my words as I claim Signy as mine once again.

She wraps her arms around my neck and sags into me.

Colin crouches beside me and kisses her neck while

Garrett stands above her, murmuring words of love in her hair.

Moments later, we rise to find the crew left to give us privacy.

Just as well, since Garrett scoops Signy into his arms and carries her to the sunbed where we spend the rest of the evening making stars burst before her eyes.

igny

"WE'RE a week away from Moen Island off the coast of North Carolina. Look there. Those are the Outer Banks islands. Do you want to stop by?"

"We can go to this local bar we usually stop at on the way north."

"They have some of the best crab, shrimp"—Garrett slides up behind me, spanning his sizable hands flat on my lower belly, pressing my back against his front—"and oysters. You know what they say about oysters."

I giggle and grind back against him.

"Hmmm… They're tough to crack?" I ask coyly.

Fingers slide down to cup my pussy while the heel of his hand adds pressure to my clit. I moan as my head lolls back against his chest. The long middle finger slips beneath my bikini bottom. It glides along my slick slit. My chest rises on heavy pants as he twirls the tip just inside my pussy.

"Mmmm… Yes. But they're known as aphrodisiacs," he rasps as his cock thickens and lengthens at my back. "But you don't need them. Do you?"

I whimper as he increases the depth of his finger and the pressure on my clit.

"No. You don't. Not with your soaking wet pussy," he growls.

"You're always so ready for us, Little Wolf," Colin groans as he kneels before me.

I mewl as his tongue joins Garrett's finger. It laps at the juices coating my lower lips, staying just out of reach where I need his tongue the most. My hips undulate, aligning my clit with his mouth. I cry out as he latches onto the sensitive bud and sucks. The lewd sloppy wet sounds of his mouth on my pussy and Garrett's fingers thrusting deep inside draw out a toe-curling orgasm.

I scream my pleasure, not caring who hears my passion. My back arches as Dolph's mouth engulfs my tit. His tongue flicks rapidly across the puckered tip. My eyes roll to the back of my head as another orgasm rocks my core. My pussy walls clench on Garrett's fingers as I gush into Colin's mouth. I wail and shake violently.

"No. You don't need oysters," Garrett growls as his other hand moves against my back.

A keen rips from my throat as he rams his giant cock

into my tight pussy with one brutal thrust. A savage growl sends shivers down my spine as he grips my hip to hold me still for his pistoning strokes.

My mind leaves me as he uses my body while Dolph and Colin lavish me with their wicked tongues. Wave after wave of carnal pleasure rolls over me. My knees give out, only for Colin to boost me up for more of their feral assault.

"Take me, Signy! Take all of me!" Garrett barks as a torrent of hot cum shoots into my womb.

No sooner does the last spurt fill me does Colin hoist me in the air. Automatically, my legs wind around his narrow waist. He lifts me higher, then drops me down to impale my pussy with his turgid length. I wail as he roars my name.

More hands grip my waist. Another fat dick nudges at my puckered hole. My head thrashes as Dolph works his cock into my ass. The ring of muscles resists but gives way at his insistence. The broad head pops past, followed by his thick length until he bottoms out. Balls brush the crease of my ass.

The three of us groan at the snug fit.

"Fuck, baby... So damn good..."

"You take your mates so well, Little Wolf."

A hand grabs mine and wraps it around a third hard cock. I tighten my grip and pump up and down, squeezing along the shaft.

"Hell yeah, baby," Garrett rasps. "Just like that."

His hips jut as I increase the speed.

"Cum for us, Signy… Cum for us now!" Colin roars as he shoots his load deep into my womb.

Dolph grunts as Colin's dick grows larger, consuming more space in my little pussy. With a guttural groan, Dolph releases ropes of cum inside my ass. It drips out to the deck, joining the excess of Colin's eruption.

My pussy and ass clench at the burn and stretch of their cocks filling both my holes at the same time. I cum with a silent scream even as Garrett's dick jettisons hot cum on my hand. He roars as he bucks through his climax.

Dolph's cock pops out as Colin lowers to the floor, still filling my pussy. He positions me on his lap, straddling his hips and presses kisses to the side of my neck to the dip of my collarbone. His warm breath slides across my sweat-drenched skin.

I shudder from the aftershocks of the explosive orgasm. My boneless body sags against him as I drift off in carnal bliss.

Garrett

"YOU DIDN'T THINK we'd forget to feed you. Did you?"

Dolph asks Signy as we ride in the tender headed to the bar.

She slept for over an hour after our last *ocean-deep fucking,* as she likes to call it. But our baby needs to eat.

Colin ate her out, waking her with another orgasm. Dolph bathed her in the shower, and I had the pleasure of massaging oil into her supple skin.

She joked about how we spoil her. But that's our goal. Keep Our Queen happy.

Now, she beams at Dolph.

"No. I know you'll aways take care of me," she says and turns to Colin and me. "All of you. And I can't wait to devour some seafood. Even oysters!"

We laugh as she grins at me.

Colin navigates the tender to the dock in front of the bar. I hop out and tie the boat off, then extend my hands to Signy. Dolph holds her hips as I lift her onto the dock.

"Thank you, kindly," she says as she loops an arm through mine.

Dolph and Colin follow as we head up the dock and across the lawn to the two-story bar.

The ground-floor patio buzzes with music from the live band and people dancing. We take the stairs on the side to the upper deck. A hostess greets us, and I request an outdoor table next to the railing so we can watch the sunset and listen to the music.

As she leads us to a table, we pass a group of human males seated at two tables. One male notices our approach and nudges another. Their eyes fixate on Signy.

The white strapless mini dress shows off her tan and lithe body. A gust of wind catches her hair, and she tosses it over her shoulder, laughing at something Colin said. Oblivious, she strides right past the table of gawking males.

My hands fist as I glare at them. My wolf snarls, baring his fangs. Tongue flicks in warning.

"Here you go."

The hostess stops at the table next to theirs and places the menus on top.

"No," I snarl, then catch myself when her eyes widen. "We'd prefer the one in the corner, if you don't mind."

Dolph, Colin.

I speak to them through my Alpha bond.

What's up?

Those fuckers are leering at our mate.

Colin turns to face the humans as Dolph steps beside him.

"You're not looking at her, right?" Colin asks as he towers over their table. Undetectable to the human eye, his body increases in mass as he partially shifts.

Signy pauses. But I place a hand at the small of her back, urging her on to our table.

Dolph, Colin, please don't get into it with those humans. We should just leave.

She uses our bond to defuse the situation.

But nothing will satisfy our wolves until the human males back off. We won't fully shift, only let them witness enough of our strength to think twice about ogling our mate. Our instinct to protect her intensifies.

The humans glance amongst themselves. The one closest to Dolph raises his hands, palms out.

"No dude, just happened to look up when she passed by.

Nothing more," he says, eyes darting between Dolph and Colin.

"Yeah. All good. All right?" Another adds.

"As long as you keep it to 'nothing.' *Dude*." Colin snarls. He eyes each one until they lower their gazes, then he pivots.

"Enjoy your evening," Dolph says. His fierce expression belies his words as he glares at each one and stalks away.

I watch standing behind Signy's chair with my hands on her shoulders until Dolph and Colin reach our table. The first guy scowls at their backs until his gaze lifts to mine. My eyes narrow to slits as the corner of my lip lifts. He flinches and drops his gaze. I continue to glare at him until they sit, and Signy places a hand on mine.

"If we're staying, please sit, my love. Don't let them ruin our night. Okay?" She asks, tilting her head up to look at me with imploring eyes.

I flick my gaze back at the fucker. Satisfied he's not looking this way, I squeeze Signy's shoulders and drop into the chair next to her. My hand rests on her thigh possessively.

"Okay, baby. All good."

She smiles sweetly and places her hand on top of mine.

"Yes, 'all good.' Because you know"—she slides our joined hands up her thigh and beneath her mini dress to press them against her soaked pussy—"this pussy is yours. Dolph's. And. Colin's."

For each name, she presses my fingers past her wet, swollen folds and glances at each of us.

"Man… Don't make me jump over this table, grab you, and run back to the tender. Dinner be damned," Colin says gruffly.

"I don't need to see what you're doing. I can scent your musky arousal, Little Wolf," Dolph growls and adjusts his seat.

She grins and crosses her legs, locking my hand to her pussy. I scissor my fingers, stretching her to add another. Her hips gyrate as her thighs squeeze.

The three of us groan when she lifts her hand to her mouth and, one by one, licks her slick fingers clean. Her eyes flutter close on a sultry moan.

"Would you say the food here is as good as my pussy?"

Colin chokes on a sip of water. The glass tinkles as it knocks against the utensils.

Dolph sits gobsmacked. Eyes dart from her fingers to her mouth.

I reach over and grip the side of her neck, tugging her towards me. My mouth crashes over hers. My tongue laps inside to taste the remnants of her sweet juices. She leans into me, moaning wantonly. Having captured the flavor, I sit back and smirk at her flushed face, breathless from my kiss.

"You tease. I take, Little Wolf."

She inhales deeply and leans back in her chair. Sparkling eyes sweep around the table.

"Shall we order?"

I throw my head back and laugh at her cheekiness. I slip my fingers from her hot pussy and lick them clean.

Colin wipes his shirt while Dolph gestures for the server.

The human female saunters over. Her eyes rake over Dolph as her lips curl up in a seductive smile.

"What will you have, handsome?"

"Not. You."

The server blinks at Signy's savage snarl. Her eyes widen when Signy leans forward.

"It's rude to flirt with another female's male"—she flicks her eyes to the name tag on the server's cropped top—"*Gladys.*"

Gladys' mouth opens and closes like a fish gasping for air, unable to form words.

"*We'll* have three seafood towers with an extra dozen oysters," Signy says, then smiles sweetly. "Thank you, Gladys."

She nods and scurries away on sky-high platforms.

"You're not the only possessive ones," Signy adds with a smirk. "You are all mine and mine alone, babes. Mine."

My cock thickens down my thigh.

Colin crouches beside her chair and stares up at her, eyes glowing.

"Say it again."

"You. Are. All. Mine. And. Mine. Alone."

He closes his eyes and groans in the back of his throat.

"Sexy as fuck," Dolph rumbles.

I rub the back of her neck, enraptured by our mate.

Colin grips her thighs as he rises, then sits on his chair.

"When we return to the boat, promise you'll show just how much we're yours, Little Wolf," he says.

"I absolutely promise."

Servers—other than Gladys—bring the mountains of seafood and extra oysters. The four female humans avert their eyes as they place the towers on the table and hurry away. Two return with frosty pitchers of beer and chilled mugs. They nod and leave. Obviously, Gladys warned them about the ferocious female.

Signy snickers, popping a shrimp in her mouth. Her eyes close on a moan.

"You are so right… This is delicious," she says, smacking her lips and reaching for a lobster claw.

"Not as good as you. But glad you like it," I say and swipe warm melted butter from the corner of her mouth and popping the finger in my mouth. "Mmm… Tasty Signy."

She giggles, and we eat.

By the time we finish, the sun set in a fiery ball and a new band takes over. Signy insists we dance and heads to the ladies' room while we find a table near the packed dance floor. Women give us the eye and a few of them drop by. But as much as we adore Possessive Signy, we don't want a bar brawl. We decline their advances.

"Where could Signy—"

An angry yell of our names blasts across our mate bond. We leap to our feet and dart around the other tables. With each step, our wolves threaten to burst forth to track down whomever dares to upset our fated mate. We ignore the grumblings of the patrons as we push past them, following her scent.

We find her in the dark area behind the bar, surrounded by the human males from upstairs. Back against the wall, she strikes out at them with fingernails elongated enough to shred flesh but not full claws.

"Don't touch me, asshole!"

"You fuck three guys. Well, here's your chance to fuck six."

The fucker who first stared at her steps forward, unbuckling his belt.

A red haze descends over my vision. My bones crack and realign. With a predatory roar, my wolf breaks free. One leap, and I pounce on the fucker.

His squeal turns into a bloody gurgle as my fangs grip his throat and my head jerks sideways. He collapses in a heap at my paws. I swing around, placing my body between Signy and the rest of the cowards. Snarling, my massive body vibrates. A paw swipes out to slash the face of another human male. He drops.

The acrid scent of piss mixed with fear fills the air.

A couple scramble backwards, only to turn and face the jaws of a tawny wolf. The others fall under the paws of a golden wolf.

Within two minutes, we eliminate the threat.

Signy, stay out of sight and get back to the tender. Bring it north of the bar. We'll meet you there in fifteen minutes.

Colin inclines his head towards his ripped jeans.

Without questioning me, she nods, retrieves the tender's ignition key, and slips through the shadows.

Years of training come into use as we clear the area. We shift and gather our torn clothes, then carry two bodies each through a wooded area to an inlet leading to the ocean. We dump the dead fuckers in the water, leaving them for the bull sharks to feast on. Blending into the darkness, we make our way to Signy.

CHAPTER 14

igny

"So, you're into foursomes, are you?"

The hairs on the back of my neck stand on end. My wolf jumps to her feet, hackles raised and teeth bared as a warning growl rises from her throat.

For a second, I freeze, caught in a flashback to my kidnapping by Blaise's men. Helplessness washes over me as the phantom sensation of zip ties digging into my wrists reappears. Unconsciously, I rub the unblemished skin.

I startle as a hand clamps over my mouth and my legs go out from under me.

Once again, I'm flung over the man's shoulder. My arms dig into my ribs and my belly. The air whooshes from my lungs. A crack to my ass jolts me to the present.

"We'll show you an even better time."

Malicious laughter and lewd comments follow his statement.

My mouth opens. My fangs elongate. They clamp on his ass, easily ripping through the denim. I fall to the ground as he yells.

Blood fills my mouth.

I crab-walk backwards until I hit a wall, then slide up to my feet, hands braced on the stone behind me.

"You bitch!"

"You have no idea," I snarl, swiping a hand over my mouth. The metallic taste of his blood churns my stomach.

Garrett! Dolph! Colin!

I scream for them through our bond.

Another human male lunges towards me. His fingertips brush the curve of my breast. I bat him away, scratching his hand with lengthened claws. My instinct to protect myself doesn't override the need to maintain as much of my human appearance as possible. They won't think twice about the bite and the scratches.

"Get away from me, or you'll regret it."

They glance at each other and laugh. Another one darts froward, and I jump sideways, spinning and kicking his knee. He yelps and hobbles back.

"Don't touch me, asshole!"

"You fuck three guys. Well, here's your chance to fuck six."

The one I guess as their leader steps forward. He winks and licks his lips as he loosens his belt.

One second he's leering at me, and the next, a blur of jet black fur rips his throat out. He falls dead. The rest succumb to the fury of my mates as their wolves attack in an animalistic display of pure testosterone.

Some may call them monsters and loathe them.

I watch, fascinated.

My mates' enormous wolves move with the grace and the lethal cunning of apex predators. Muscles ripple beneath their fur as their powerful jaws snap and huge paws slash. Silently, they cut the human males down. Not one of them has the chance to escape.

Good.

They tried it with me. How many other females have they attacked? I feel zero pity for them.

Signy, stay out of sight and get back to the tender. Bring it north of the bar. We'll meet you there in fifteen minutes.

Garrett's command breaks through my musings. Colin motions to his torn jeans.

I nod and grab the tender's ignition key from what was the front pocket, then merge with the shadows, staying out of patrons' sight at the bar.

Fortunately, the loud music and raucous atmosphere captured their attention. No one would bother to come around the back in the dark. Not when the fun is on the other side.

I don't encounter anyone as I hurry to the dock. Quickly, I unwind the mooring line from the metal cleat and toss it into the tender, hopping aboard. The ignition purrs to life. I navigate away from the dock and north to meet Garrett, Dolph, and Colin.

Fifteen minutes feel like hours. The tender idles, swaying with the waves returning from the shoreline. Only the sound of the water lapping against the boat reaches my ears. I glance up, whispering a prayer to the gods, they're fine and on their way to me. Usually an expanse of glittering stars, dance above. Tonight, clouds roll in from the Atlantic Ocean, painting an inky sky. Perfect to conceal the encounter and its aftermath.

A stronger wave rocks the tender.

I spin to find Garrett hoisting himself over one edge while Colin climbs over from the other side. Dolph follows as they pile onto the tender. I rush from the wheel to check them.

"Are you all right? No one saw you? What did you do with them?" I ask rapid fire.

Colin grips the back of my neck and tilts my head back for a quick kiss as he passes me on his way to the helm. Dolph pulls me onto the leather bench between him and Garrett. The ignition starts, and we leave the coast behind.

"Yes. No. Shark food," Garrett answers as he pulls me against his chest and buries his face in my hair.

Dolph's hands skim my arms and legs.

"Did they hurt you?" He growls.

"No. They bragged about what they planned to do to me," I say and shudder.

Dolph rubs my back and asks, "How did they get you back there?"

I explain how I left the ladies' room and stepped into an alcove to scroll through text messages when they snatched me. Garrett hisses when I tell them about my PTSD reaction. I rub his arm and shake my head.

"I'm okay. Just caught unawares. Don't worry," I say, then grin. "Besides, you guys saved me. Again. Thank you."

Dolph tsks and tells me no need to thank them. Their responsibility is to protect me. He mutters how he should have gone with me to the ladies' room. But I remind him, it's not for males and smirk. He grimaces at my lame joke.

My stomach cramps, and I gasp.

"What's the matter?"

"What happened?"

"I thought you said they didn't hurt you."

Another cramp robs the words from my mouth. I double over and groan, my arms wrap around my middle. Dolph pulls me sideways to lay my head in his lap with my legs across Garrett's thighs. A third pang hits me, and I curl into a fetal position.

"Oh, brother," I groan. "My period is coming early. Sorry."

Of all the times to change. Why during our honeymoon?

When we reach *Blue Moon*, Garrett carries me to the primary cabin.

"Nooo! I need space."

He hesitates, then pivots and strides to a nearby guest cabin suite. Dolph opens the door, and steps aside for

Garrett to walk through. Then follows with Colin. Gently, Garrett lays me on the bed. They stare down at me like I'm a slide beneath a microscope.

Frowns mar their handsome faces as their gazes scan me from head to toe.

"Do you need—"

"No! I just need space," I snap, then widen my eyes, surprised by the forcefulness of my tone. "I mean, it's embarrassing—"

"Don't. It's natural," Dolph says, eyes softened with concern. "If you need us, we'll be in the other cabins."

"Uh, yeah. We don't share a bed without you," Colin adds, dipping his eyebrows. "I'll be next door. Call if you need anything."

He leans over and kisses my forehead before he leaves.

"Are you sure you don't want Chef to fix some tea or something?" Garrett asks.

I bite back a snarl and shake my head.

He nods and presses a kiss to my lips.

"Sweet dreams, Little Wolf," he murmurs and strides from the cabin.

I glance up at Dolph.

He watches me in silence for a moment, then sits beside me. He places a hand on the inside of my ankle and presses. I moan from the pressure on the right point. Relief washes over me, and I sag against the pillows.

"How did you know to do that?" I pant.

"After your last period, I studied methods to ease pain

from cramps," he answers with a shrug. "I would offer to stay. But I'll give you your space. Just apply pressure here for ten seconds every so often."

I nod, and he leans over to kiss my lips.

"And don't worry about anyone ever taking you from us again. We will end anyone who threatens you," he says with a growl. "Now, rest. We'll see you in the morning."

"Thank you," I whisper.

Once he shuts the door behind him, I drag myself from the bed and shower. No spotting. So, I crawl into bed naked. Sleep overcomes me moments later.

The next morning, I wake twisted in sweaty sheets. Caught around my legs, I kick the clinging silk, trying to free myself.

"Aargh! Get. Off. Me!"

I roll half off the bed, hands brace on the carpet with legs tangled in the sheets. The air conditioning barely cools my bare ass sticking up in the air. I blow a breath to move the hair from my face, only for gravity to win. The long strands fall, covering my eyes again.

"Dammit!"

The door bangs open.

My head jerks up. But my stupid hair blocks my view.

"I swear, I'll cut it all off!"

"What the hell?"

"Are you all right?"

"Who we cuttin', boo?"

I buck my legs and fall completely with a grunt.

Instantly, they crouch around me. Hands touching.

"No!" I exclaim, swatting them away like gnats. "I'm fine. Hot. But fine. And it's my hair I'll cut."

I swipe it behind my ears and glare at them.

"Is this what you call giving me space?" I glance at each one. "Hmmm?"

They swallow audibly and jump to their feet. Dolph pulls me to mine while Garrett uncoils the snake sheets from my right calf. Free at last, I stalk to the bathroom, tossing a thanks over my shoulder before I shut the door.

One glance in the mirror confirms I look like a wild woman. Hair ratty around my head. Face crimson with pillow creases on a cheek. Lips and mouth dry. Sweat coats my body.

"Aargh!"

I pivot on my heel. But a cramp twists my gut until I bend over and groan, desperate for relief. Once the pain subsides, I hop on one leg to the shower as I press my other ankle. The shit doesn't work. At. All.

My palm slaps the fancy showerhead controls until the temperature and jets I want kick in. Eyes closed, I tilt my head back, allowing the cold water to soak my heated flesh. A satisfied moan slips past my cracked lips.

I greet a gentle knock on the door with my irritated, "Go away!"

Without another disturbance, I drop onto the cool marble bench and let the soothing water work its magick. I don't know how much time passed. But I awake to being carried, bundled in a cushy robe.

A cushy robe that grates my skin. Skin that's once again scorching.

My eyes pop open as I snarl and flail my arms and legs.

"Nooo! Take it off and put me down."

"Babe, we thought you were drowning in there—"

"*Grrrrr…*"

Dolph halts mid-sentence and mid-stride.

"Ooh-kay… Still need your space. All righty then," he says and lowers me to my feet.

He backs away slowly, hands warding off the expected slaps. He glances at Garrett and Colin, who know by now not to say a word. All three back out of the cabin.

Good.

I yank the offending robe off and throw it to the floor. If another cramp didn't hit me like a freight train, I would have stomped on it. Instead, I throw myself onto the cool marble floor of the bathroom and sob.

Okay, the shower may have been risky. But nothing is wrong with sleeping on the floor. Well, maybe some would find it crazy. But I find it refreshing.

I mutter a curse at suffering the worse case of PMS in history. I fall asleep bemoaning the horrible situation ruining the rest of my honeymoon.

A few hours later, I wake to find on the vanity a silver platter of freshly cut melons, pineapples, and mangos with a cluster of frozen grapes. Next to it, bottles of water float in an ice bath with frosty crystal glasses. A cream envelope with my name written in calligraphy on it leans against the mirror.

A twinge of guilt sweeps over me at the kindness of my mates, despite my snappish behavior. I rise from the floor and pop a grape in my mouth, then open the envelope.

Dearest Signy,

We respect you need space—although we must admit our confusion by your behavior—and will wait for you to come to us.

But you must eat.

Enjoy these cooling fruits (Dolph's idea, naturally). They will hydrate your cells to lower your body temperature and decrease inflammation.

With all our love,
Garrett, Dolph, and Colin

I laugh out loud at what I thought would be a love note. But follow their command. I take the platter and settle back on the floor. After gorging on the fruit and washing it down with the water, my body feels refreshed enough to seek my mates.

I slip on a silk robe. Immediately, the fabric suffocates me. With a frustrated growl, I rip it off and stomp towards the door.

The moment I open it and step into the hallway, my nostrils flare.

Enticing sandalwood and vanilla.

Comforting musky masculine.

Heady leather, spices, and musk.

A shudder rocks my entire body.

My knees buckle as the worse cramp ever tears through my lower belly. Fever hits me, spiking my body temperature. Sweat breaks out above my upper lip, on my scalp, my underarms, every-damn-where. I slap a palm against the wall to hold myself steady. My head lolls as a whimper falls from my mouth. Hair blinds me.

A deep inhalation draws more of my mates' unique scents into my nose. I hum out a moan as their scents travel through my body and ignite in my lower belly. It convulses again. Wetness gushes from my core, coating my thighs.

"No spotting? Straight on? Oh gods, it hurts!"

A sickly sweet aroma wafts up as more wetness slicks my inner thighs and puddles on the floor.

I whimper and turn for the bathroom. My foot slips, and I tumble to the floor. The sweet aroma increases as my hands land in the puddle, splattering it around me.

My mouth drops when I see an unexpected substance dripping from my fingers.

"*Aroo!*"

I freeze as three feral howls combine to rend the air. My eyes squeeze shut.

From three directions, feet pound the floor. My body vibrates with each step. The howls increase as they draw closer. Mewls slip from my mouth. Nearby, heavy breathing raises goosebumps on my sweat-drenched skin. I shiver despite the fever. Air drawn deeply into three noses escapes in one word.

"*Maaate...*"

igny

WAS IT THE APHRODISIAC OYSTERS? Or was it the captivating display of brutal masculine possessiveness? Three virile male wolf shifters protecting their mate? Whatever the cause, it brought on my heat. Intensely. Unexpectedly. Hard.

As my wolf prances to a stop and lifts her tail, I realize it was my mates' prowess that triggered my heat. As with all animals, they mate with the strongest to ensure the continuation of the species. Survival of the fittest.

Such as what happened with my wolf. She needed visual proof our mates are vital enough to carry on the next line. Capable of filling my womb with potent seed to create strong pups who will grow to Alphas or Lunas.

Sure, she knows they're Green Berets, big, powerful. But she never witnessed them in action. Even when they rescued me, it was only the aftermath she saw.

But the other night?

Another cramp grips my core. Slick gushes and drips between my clenched thighs. The sickly sweet aroma thickens in the tense air.

Oh, gods!

"Mate!"

"Wait!" I wail in a panic as a sense of not being ready hits me. My eyes dart around.

The hallway. This isn't right!

"Space! I need—"

"No. More. Space!"

I scurry backwards as the three of them descend on me. Lust-crazed faces loom. Hands reach out. I shake my head violently and scream. They freeze. Heads cock. Eyebrows raise.

"Nest... I *must* fix my nest," I plead, tears streaming down my face. "I'm not ready..."

Dolph's face softens, and he nods.

"I understand, Little Wolf. Where do you want to build your nest? I'll help you."

Colin hisses and runs his fingers through the long strands at the crown of his head. He musses them up, adding to the crazed look on his face.

Garrett fares better at my plea. He sucks in a deep breath, then shakes his head as more of my enthralling scent flows through his nostrils. His eyes flare with his wolf fighting to breach the surface. But Garrett flattens his lips and drags himself to the opposite wall. His lust-filled eyes never leave my face.

"It's best if you help her, Dolph, as you have better control than Colin and me," he says in a voice roughened with carnal desire. "But. Hurry."

Dolph lifts me to my feet. He sways as my scent floats around us. His eyes blink. A second later, he nods, more to himself than to me.

"Where?" He asks gruffly, keeping his hands fisted at his sides.

I glance down at them and back up at him.

He grimaces.

"I cannot touch you without the urge to knot you unraveling the slight thread I have on my control. *Where?*"

Instinctively, I point to the primary cabin. It was from there the lingering scents of my three mates emanated when I exited the guest cabin. I need to surround myself with their combined scents. Build my nest in the center of our space. Welcome them to me.

He gestures me ahead of him and follows. Garrett and Colin remain. Colin's grumbling shadows our steps.

Inside the cabin, my eyes search for the perfect spot. With my temperature boiling, I consider the cool bathroom tile as the base of my nest. But my wolf whines, not happy with the option. My gaze moves to the balcony. Despite it being early June, the Atlantic Ocean breeze remains chilly. I envision the stars above and the four of us below on a plethora of soft pillows and cozy blankets. My wolf's whine heightens.

As though my wolf moves me, my feet hurry to the massive bed. My hands reach out to touch the cashmere throw draped across the foot of the bed. Immediately, a sense of just right fills me. I feel like Goldilocks once she finds the one bed for her. My wolf drops to her back and wiggles her body as if the soft cashmere glides across her fur.

Perfect!

"Here. Right here," I mutter to myself as I run my hands over the new cover. The staff must have changed the bedding since the four of us last slept here. It's clear Garrett stayed in a guest suite, too. "But it needs more."

I glance around as I pace every inch of the cabin.

The scent of them grows stronger at the walk-in closet. I slide the door open and hurry inside.

Enticing sandalwood and vanilla.

Comforting musky masculine.

Heady leather, spices, and musk.

I mewl as I grab T-shirts, pulling them to my nose and inhaling deeply. My belly cramps and fresh slick gushes from my pussy. I squeeze my thighs together and dance on tippy toe, moaning as I strive for relief.

"Fuck! Do. Not. Do. That."

Colin's ferocious growl catches me by surprise. I yelp and pull the T-shirts from my face, staring at him with wide eyes.

"S—Sorry," I whimper, even as more slick drips to my knees.

"Hurry, Signy…"

I nod repeatedly like a marionette pulled by strings.

"O-Okay. Yes."

With a sweep of my hands over the neat stacks, I gather more of their clothing and rush to the bed. Slick drips behind me, leaving a sickly sweet trail. Colin's forceful inhalations and low growls spur me on.

I must fix my nest!

An oversized decorative pillow on the floor by the balcony catches my eye. I toss the clothing on the bed and hurry over to grab it. Once I fluff it to my chest, I place it in the center of the bed. I crawl after it and plump the other pillows. As I sit back on my haunches, I critique my work.

Not enough!

My hands move in a frenzy as I pull the precisely tucked cover and sheets to form a heap around the big pillow. I rearrange the silk pillows against the headboard in a semicircle. My head tilts as I consider the changes.

My eyes narrow.

Too much light.

"Dolph, dim the overhead lights and lower the blackout shades!"

He grumbles about, hurrying up. But stalks to the wall and adjusts the system's panel. The shades lower, and a soft glow fills the room.

"Better?"

His growl liquifies my knees.

I collapse in the middle of my perfect nest. A mewl falls from my mouth as my hips gyrate. Nipples tighten to sensitive points. A flush suffuses my entire body. Heat pools in my lower belly. It constricts painfully. More slick pours from my desperate pussy.

"Yes... Yes... *Yes!*"

The door slams against the wall.

I gasp as my eyes snap to the doorway. Heart beats wildly against my ribs.

A naked Garrett stands there. Chest rises and falls with his ragged pants. Fists clench. Wild eyes darkened to cobalt blue with lust scan the cabin until they land on my hooded ones. The room pulsates with erotic energy as he storms in.

"Now, Mate. Now!"

I double over as a cramp steals my breath. I pant, arms tightening around my middle. Scorching heat blazes across my sweat-drenched skin. The pounding of my heart echoes in my ears. Eyes squeeze shut. Red-hot sparks burst before my closed lids.

"Alpha... Need... you..."

Garrett bounds across the floor. Sandalwood and vanilla engulf me. I mewl pitifully. The bed dips under his weight. Calloused hands grab my waist and flip me onto my belly. The breath whooshes from my lungs as my chest collides with the mattress.

He grips my hips and yanks my ass into the air. My entire body lifts, light as a feather. I scramble to put my palms on the bed. My knees lower. He uses one of his knees to knock my thighs apart. One hand digs into the flesh of my hip as the other moves away.

I whine as the bulbous head of his giant cock breaches my swollen folds, slick with my heat. I scream and thrash as he drives into my tight pussy with one brutal thrust. An orgasm rips through me at the intense burn of his ginormous cock stretching and filling me. A strangled cry falls from my mouth.

Slick gushes to coat his dick and eases the way as he withdraws and slams back in. Our animalistic grunts and growls rise into the air, along with the combined scent of slick, sweat, and pheromones.

I take what he gives me, bouncing on his cock like a rag doll.

"*Back. Off!*" Garrett thunders.

Colin growls.

"She's our mate too."

Garrett ignores Colin's complaint and intensifies the snapping of his hips. The bed rocks with each forceful thrust. He binds an arm around my waist and lowers his heaving chest to my back. The other hand drops onto mine. Our fingers entwine. The warmth of his breath against my neck flames, the fire flickering across my skin. Lips press a guttural groan to my slick flesh.

"*Fuuuck*… the gods made you for me… every thick inch fills your perfect pussy."

"*Oh, gods!*"

"Not, gods. *Your mate.* I'm going to fill your womb with my seed. Put my pup in your belly."

Heat ignites in my lower belly. My pussy walls convulse, squeezing along his length, milking his cock for its potent seed.

"Yes!" He bellows, jackhammering into my core.

The rhythmic slapping of his groin pounding my ass fills the cabin. In the distance, I hear barbaric growls from Dolph and Colin. Curses pour from their mouths with each of Garrett's thrusts. My carnal cries join them.

"Uh. Uh. Uh. Uh."

As if he weren't wrecking my pussy enough, Garrett collars my throat and yanks our torsos up. My back crashes against his sweaty chest. He leans on his haunches with the backs of my thighs resting on his. The muscles ripple beneath me. My hands grapple at his ass, taut as he pumps up relentlessly. His cock rails my pussy.

But it's not enough.

"*More!* More, dammit!"

My head thrashes from side to side as I beg him to fuck me harder. For my Alpha to satisfy my aching need for him to fill my womb with his seed. I whine with need, blabbering incoherently.

"I'm going to fuck you through your heat until my seed takes root," he snarls.

He hoists me off his lap. His cock slips from my pussy. I wail at the loss, only to yelp as he flips me to my back and plunges back in. My knees meet my ears as he folds me in half and drills me into the mattress.

"Ohhhh…"

More slick leaks from my pussy. I beg him for more.

Garrett growls low and husky as his cock swells at the base. He continues to pound into me as the size increases. He forces it deeper, locking behind my pelvic wall.

I scream.

"Take my knot and my seed."

My mind and body fight the fiery stretch. But my wolf howls in carnal delight as his cock floods my womb with his life-giving essence. There's no question Garrett is an Alpha more than strong enough to ensure the continuation of wolf shifters.

The thought triggers another soul-stealing orgasm. It starts at the tips of my toes and skitters along every nerve ending. Spasms vibrate through my legs, knocking them against his arms bracketing my head. I gasp as the shock-wave threads through my core. My pussy contracts. I shake beneath him, crying out his name.

He grunts as my pussy envelops his cock like a fist. It pulses as the last of his seed empties into me. The weight of his body presses me further into my nest as his elbows bend. The long strands of his damp hair caress my face and throat as he buries his face in the crook of my neck. Heavy, hot pants fan over my wet skin. He groans as my pussy sucks him in deeper.

"So tight… So good… So mine," he growls in a deep and dark voice.

I welcome his weight atop me. My legs lower as my arms loop under his to rest on his back. I tug him close to me and sigh. Pussy sated as his knot locks us together to ensure his seed stays in my womb to root.

"Aaaahhh..."

"Ohhh, *fuck!*"

The blissful moment gets blasted as Dolph and Colin bellow through their climaxes. The musky scent of their releases mingles with the heavy aroma of animalistic sex.

Instinctively, my pussy clenches at the erotic sounds of my other mates.

Garrett grunts and wraps his arms around me. He rolls to his back, draping me over his big body. His knot stays in place.

I glance over my shoulder to find Dolph and Colin naked, kneeling at the foot of the bed. Fists grip their engorged dicks. Ropes of cum paint the cashmere throw. I lick my lips, sorry to not have devoured their cream. Heavy-lidded eyes glow with their wolves present as their gazes lock on me tighter than Garrett's knot. My lower belly cramps with more slick. The aroma rises between us.

Their nostrils flare. Chests expand on deep inhalations. Eyebrows slash over their dilated eyes. They growl in unison.

"As soon as Garrett's knot releases you, I'm going to fuck that heat right out of you," Dolph snarls, stroking his thickening cock.

"And I'm taking that tight ass," Colin barks.

I whimper, undulating my hips.

Garrett squeezes each cheek, spreading my ass open for all to see.

My puckered hole contracts greedily, even as I turn and hide my face against his chest. I have no control over my body. The urge for each of my holes to be filled, mounted, and plundered savagely robs me of reason. I tremble with need.

"We will satisfy you until your heat ends with our pup secure in your belly. Do not hide from your body's nature. Do you understand, Little Wolf?"

He rumbles to soothe me.

"Y—Yes, Alpha," I whisper in a voice hoarse from my screams.

"Good, girl."

My pussy vibrates, ready for more.

And I love it.

CHAPTER 16

olph

My dick hurts.

It literally hurts.

Along with my balls.

I didn't even realize they could shrink.

"Oh, Colin! Right there... Yes. Yes. *Yes!*"

"Fuck my big dick like you really need it, Little Wolf!"

My cock and balls shrivel.

Even through the closed bathroom door and over the shower's running water from eight jets, Signy's frantic cries reach me. Colin's responding roar could shatter the vanity mirror. Damn my enhanced hearing.

I scrub a hand down my face and groan, not in pleasure.

Six days, five nights, twelve hours of nonstop fucking.

Signy is insatiable. Her greedy cunt soaks up our cum like a sponge. Garrett's knot loosens, and she's reaching for me. I bang her mercilessly, and she begs for Colin. We make it our mission to quench her heat. But the damn thing never ends. It has her in a tizzy and us right along with her.

Never in my life would I imagine not wanting pussy.

With a drawn-out groan, my head tilts back for the rain shower to cascade over my sweaty body.

I just finished my last round with Signy and need to wash our sweat and her slick from my clammy skin. The water sluices over the angular planes of my face, down my sculpted pecs and over the ridges of my eight-pack abs. My cock twitches with relief at the fresh water's brisk contact. My ball sac draws upwards, as though trying to escape back inside of my body.

I turn and brace my palms on the shower's marble wall. Its coolness seeps in to ease the internal furnace fueled by Signy's pleas for *more, more, more*. I can no more deny my mate's need for me than I can ignore Garrett's Alpha command. My nature as a beta wolf shifter will not allow it.

In my mind's eye, my wolf glances up at me. If he were human, he'd nod and empathize with me. Instead, he stares with drained eyes. Days before, he was baying with glee to mate. Well…

I reach for the sea sponge and drip lavender and peppermint bodywash on it. My muscles thank me as I massage the soothing gel on my aching limbs. Talk about a workout. I feel like I'm in bootcamp and crawled on my belly beneath a ceiling of barbed wire from Moen Island to San Diego. Signy's demands push my stamina to the limits. Who knew a she-wolf's heat could topple even the fittest male wolf shifter?

My head shakes as more garbled cries penetrate the bathroom.

Despite my body's worn state, blood shoots south to fill my cock. Nature demands I breed my mate, even if my body aches.

I cock my head to listen for sounds of Garrett.

He's hellbent on impregnating Signy. Early morning, late night, sunrise, sundown, he fucks her until her heat subsides. In her nest, against the wall, on the balcony, everywhere, but the shower. He reeks of sex. His entire body suffused with the honey sweet scent of her heat mingled with her unique scent and his pheromones. She's covered in his scent. No one would wonder who she's mated to. His Alpha status will allow nothing less than her womb nurturing his pup, continuing the Moen line.

He only reins in his libido enough for me to feed and to bathe her. His one-track mind focuses on his progeny.

My beta brain ensures Signy's basic needs, along with her being comfortable despite the carnal torment of her heat. I'm the one who carries her limp body to the bathtub and cleanses the sweat and sex from her skin, then massage soothing oils over her sore limbs. Detangle her waist-length hair, shampoo, and condition it before drying the silky strands or braiding them. Keep her hydrated and fed.

She only trusts me to provide fresh bedding or our

clothes for her *perfect* nest. During my off-Signy rotation, I scour *Blue Moon* for items she would want against her sensitive and hot skin. My heart soars with her delighted laughter at the treasures I uncover.

And when she cries for me…

No matter how ready or weary I may be, I fall onto her like a savage beast. Our bodies rock in sync, chasing away her heat, and sating our need to mate until neither of us can move.

I drop my head on a groan as my cock stands tall. The crown bumps my navel. A pearl of pre-cum rises from the slit.

Refusing to waste a single drop, I slap the panel to stop the water and rush from the bathroom, not bothering to dry off. My eyes find Signy begging Colin for more while he lies beneath her, eyes closed. Even the bad boy has his limits.

As though sensing my presence or detecting my fresh scent, Signy's head whips around. My cock weeps as a desperate moan slips from her mouth. Arms reach out to welcome me.

A deep, passionate growl rises from my chest.

"Dolph…" she moans on a shuddering breath.

I cross the room in a few long strides and pluck her from Colin's lap. Knot deflated, his dick pops free. He grunts, and she whines with need. Her pussy gushes slick. It dribbles onto his thighs. He groans and rolls to his side.

I use her wetness to ease my way and drop her onto my eager dick. She hisses at the depth and angle of the position. I roll my hips and plow deeper still. Standing in the middle of the cabin, I fuck her until her pussy drains my sac of every drop of my seed. She groans and writhes, spearing herself even more.

As the last of my seed floods her womb, I carry her to the bathroom where we'll soak in the tub until my knot softens. The gods willing, our carnal union will end her heat. If a wolf could grin, mine would knowing our seed took root.

I guess we'll have to see.

COLIN

I SIT LAZILY STROKING my cock as I watch Garrett and Dolph double penetrate our mate into a state of sheer euphoria. All three on their knees with her smaller frame sandwiched between their much larger and partially shifted bodies, she throws her head back and screams in wild abandon. One hand claws into Garrett's shoulder while the other digs into Dolph's ass, driving them closer to her.

My eyes lock on her full tits as they bounce with each perfectly coordinated thrust. The distended nipples—a shade darker than their usual dusty pink—beg to be suckled.

As though reading my mind, Garrett dips his head and

latches on. Signy moans deep in the back of her throat and cradles his head, arching her back to offer him more of her tit. He accepts and widens his mouth to engulf the mound. His cheeks hallow out as he draws back to suck her nipple. She squeals as he growls and nips the sensitive bud. His hand cups the other tit and tugs the nipple. She moans and grinds her ass back on Dolph's groin.

He groans and fists her hair, yanking her head sideways. His mouth lowers to her throat, where he grazes the long column with his elongated fangs. She mutters curses as her body convulses with an orgasm. He and Garrett grunt.

I don't need to be buried in her pussy to know it squeezed the hell out of their dicks.

Mine thumps in my hand, still ready to fuck her raw. I tug a platinum bead on the wand of my deep shaft, reverse Prince Albert piercing and groan at the delicious bite of pain. Pre-cum drips at the slit. I rub a thumb over the warm cream and use it as natural lube. My hand jerks in time with their thrusts. Closing my eyes, I rest my head against the chair.

I allow my enhanced senses to play out the scene before me. The scent of thick musk and the honeyed aroma of her heat filters into my nostrils and bursts across my tastebuds. My mouth waters. The steady rhythm of their alternating thrusts combined with the squelching of her slick-filled pussy heat my loins. Seed fills my heavy balls. I increase the pressure along my shaft, stroking to the crown. Another tug on my piercing and my body shudders.

My ass clenches to thrust my hips and drive my cock through the tight circle of my fingers. I grunt at the same time as Garrett. My seed jettisons from my cock at the same time he erupts into Signy's womb. Dolph follows with a bellow. His seed mingles with Garrett's, each vying to take root in her fertile womb.

Signy whines as their knots swell. They rumble to soothe her. Whines morph into soft mewls as they settle on the bed, locked together in a passionate embrace.

My eyes open slowly on a sigh.

After a languorous stretch, I head to the bathroom for a much-deserved shower. Undoubtedly, Signy will need me once their knots deflate. And I'll be ready for her.

Garrett

I ROLL OVER WITH A GROAN. Every muscle, sinew, and bone in my body protests. The sheet twists around my lap. Another groan emerges as the silk brushes my limp dick nestled between my thighs. I push the sheet away and rise on an elbow to glance around the cabin.

On the opposite side of the bed, Dolph sleeps on his back, one arm thrown across his face, the other hand covers his dick. Even in sleep, his body knows to protect itself from being ravished by our insatiable mate.

The spot between us is empty of said mate. My

eyebrows dip as I cock my head to listen for her. But hear nothing from the bathroom or from the balcony. I swing my feet around and stand, stretching my arms overhead with a groan.

Movement across the cabin catches my eye.

Colin flips over on the sitting area sofa and drags a pillow over his face.

"Don't fucking wake me, man. And don't even think about lifting the blackout shades," he grumbles, burrowing beneath a cover.

I snort and stride for the bathroom.

The cabin is a mess and smells of nonstop sex for eight days. Despite Signy's best efforts, we destroyed her perfect nest. I pad over the remnants strewn across the floor. Being the possessive cavemen Thyra despises, we banned the chief steward and her staff from the cabin. No entering to clean. We only allowed them to leave trays of food and water at the door where we left the finished ones. No one could see our mate in the throes of her heat. For our eyes only.

A glance in the mirror reflects an exhausted face. Disheveled hair. Eyes bloodshot. Bags beneath them larger than Signy's set of designer luggage. Stubble grown to a full beard. I shake my head and turn for the shower.

After a full-body scrub down, shampoo, and shave, I emerge a new male. Still no sign of Signy. I slip on a pair of gray joggers and go search for our wayward mate. I pause outside the cabin door, sniffing the air for her scent. A faint trail leads me down the hallway towards the elevator. Not knowing which deck she exited on, I stop at each one and poke my head out to sniff the air.

A steward gasps in surprise on the bottom level. She clutches a basket of laundry in her hands.

"Alpha! Good morning. How may I help you?" She asks.

"Good morning, Carol. Carry on."

At the top deck, the wind blows Signy's scent from the bow. Not understanding why she would be up here alone, I jog towards her, then slow as she comes into view.

She sits cross-legged with a blanket over her shoulders on the sunbed. Her gaze towards the sunrise. Glorious yellow, gold, and orange rays spread into the blue sky. The colors dazzle across the dark blue surface of the Atlantic Ocean. A gentle breeze blows strands of her freshly washed hair. Absentmindedly, she swipes the tendrils from her beautiful face bathed in the sunrise's glow. Like the waters around the boat, a calm surrounds Signy.

I stop beside her.

"I was searching all over for you, Little Wolf. What are you doing up here by yourself this early in the morning?"

She tilts her head up to gaze at me. Her ice blue eyes—now clear of the lust fog that darkened them—shine with unshed tears. Her mouth opens, then she sinks her teeth into her bottom lip. She shakes her head.

Alarmed, I crouch and grasp her arms.

"What's wrong? Who hurt you? Where does it hurt?"

My eyes study her face as my hands cast around for injuries. The pounding of my heart deafens me. I see her mouth move. But the pulsing blood roars too loudly.

She covers my hands with hers and places them on her lower belly. Tears leak from her eyes. She sniffles.

I shake my head to clear it.

"Say it again. I didn't hear you."

She swallows and blinks away the tears.

"My heat ended."

Thank the gods!

I drop to my ass and grin.

She arches an eyebrow.

My jaw drops as I leap to my feet, pulling her up with me by our clasped hands. She giggles and nods.

Now, I gape, unable to form words.

She places our joined hands on her lower belly again and smiles through joyful tears.

"My heat is over because the three of you filled my belly with your pup."

igny

"BE careful now and watch your step, Signy."

"What? Oh, for fuck's sake!"

I bite back a giggle as Colin snaps at Dolph and scoops me from the tender.

"Why risk her slipping between the boat and the dock?" He grumbles as he carries me. "And we thought you were Mr. Take Care of Signy."

"You better not drop her. Or it'll be *your* ass," Garrett calls after us.

This time, I laugh out loud at their antics. In the two days since I told them about our pregnancy, they've morphed from virile wolf shifters to clucking hens. I can't make a move without them rumbling to soothe me or doing everything for me. Two days. I can't imagine what it'll be like for months until I give birth. And after with the pup?

I crack up. Laughing so hard, tears spill down my cheeks.

Colin stops and stares.

"Are you okay?"

"What'd you do to her?"

"Why is she crying?"

My shoulders shake with more laughter. Visions of them dashing about the mansion for bottles, diapers, and a crying pup appear behind my closed eyelids. Their eyes bug out as they run around frantically. I squeeze my thighs together to keep from peeing my panties.

"I think she's losing it," Colin responds.

My hand slaps his chest as I laugh harder. I gasp for air.

"Okay. That's enough."

"Breathe, Little Wolf."

"Let's get her home. Maybe Doc can give her something."

I wave my hand for Colin to move on as I catch my breath.

"All good… You guys crack me up. That's all."

Garrett snorts.

"Well, I'm glad we entertain you," he says wryly with a smirk.

"Yeah. Don't let us caring about you and our pup disturb you," Dolph mutters.

Colin shakes his head and increases his pace until he

stops at the SUV waiting next to Moen Island's marina. He nods at the enforcer as she opens the door, then puts me on the backseat. With a cocked eyebrow daring me to argue, he pulls the seatbelt across me and clicks it into place. He presses a kiss to my belly followed by one to my lips.

"Even on the island, you will wear your seatbelt. Understand?"

My lips twitch, ready to laugh. But I hold it back and nod.

"Words, Little Wolf. I will have your words."

"Yes, Sir."

He closes the door and rounds the front of the SUV to hop in beside me. Garrett takes the wheel while Dolph sits shotgun. They glance at me, eye the seatbelt, and nod.

"You carry our pup, Signy. Get used to us hovering," Garrett says as the other two agree.

"Oh, don't get me wrong," I say, smiling at each of them. "I love it."

"Good!" They say in unison.

I giggle and cup Colin's cheek.

"And will you go out after midnight in the rain to get my favorite ice cream or Thai food?"

"Abso-damn-lutely. Whatever our baby girl wants, we will get," he says, brushing his lips across my palm. He places a hand on my belly and spreads the fingers. "We want you and our pup more than content."

Garrett and Dolph agree, and I thank them as tears brim in my eyes.

We ride the rest of the way in a comfortable silence.

Dolph hops out and carries me from the SUV to the double doors. They open wide. My mouth drops.

"Signy!"

"Congratulations, sweetheart!"

Our family members hurry toward us, exclaiming their happiness for us being with pup. They surround us as Dolph continues inside and places me on a sofa in the great room. My mother sits beside me and pulls me into an embrace while the others gather around.

"Oh, sweetheart. What fantastic news! We're so glad your mates called to tell us to meet you home to celebrate. We flew in yesterday afternoon."

"And now, we'll party tonight!" Wren adds, ever the event planner.

"The entire pack will celebrate with us. They're so excited!" Vera says.

Natalie steps forward and smiles.

"I know you have a pack doctor. But if you want me to examine you as an OB-GYN, say the word. I'll even stay closer to your delivery."

My heart swells from their outpouring of love. Tears blur my vision.

"Babe!"

In an instant, my mates gather me in their arms. Their deep rumbling soothes me. I sniffle and smile, embarrassed by my emotional outburst.

"Forgive me. I'm so glad everyone is together to celebrate with us. What a lovely surprise. Thank you."

"No need to thank your family, little sister," Jagger says,

then flicks his gaze at my mates. "We'll talk offline about what you can expect."

Rust laughs and adds, "Yeah. Let's go back to that steakhouse. You'll need some bottles of whiskey."

The great room fills with laughter as the males nod and the she-wolves nudge them.

Even surrounded by our elated family members, my mates send waves of love through our bond. Knowing they're here to love and to care for our pup and me is all I'll ever need.

The next day, my mother, mothers-in-law, and my girls come over for *a pup planning session*, as my mother calls it. Everyone but Thyra—who's otherwise engaged—settle in the family room with cookies and tea.

"First. Did you select a room to convert into a nursery?" Sigrid asks.

Her comment at the celebration party made me think. When the four of us returned home afterwards, I asked their thoughts on the guest suite that mirrors ours for the nursery. I smile at their repeated declaration of *whatever our baby girl wants*.

"By that Cheshire Cat grin on your face, that's a definite yes," Sage says with a laugh.

I nod.

"Come. I'll show you."

We troop upstairs, and I push the double doors open with a flair.

But it's me who gasps in surprise when I find the sitting room empty and the doors to the bedroom open, revealing its furniture gone too. A fresh coat of white paint covers the soft yellow previously on the walls and on the ceiling. New simple domes replace the chandeliers and sconces. The only leftover from the original suite is the bleached hardwood floor.

Propped against the window seat is a cream envelope with my name written in calligraphy.

My smile returns as I practically skip across the sitting room.

Dearest Signy,

You do not know how happy you being pregnant with our pup makes us. First, the gods bless us with you as our fated mate. Now, you will bear our pup.

This time, it's Colin's idea to do as promised and woke us after midnight to prepare the suite for whatever design you want for our pup's nursery. Only be sure it's pup-proof.

With all our love,
Garrett, Dolph, and Colin

Emotions overwhelm me. I lower to the window seat and sob.

"Oh, honey. Your hormones are making you all teary already," Estrid says as she sits beside me and wraps an arm around my shoulders. "You might as well get used to the mood swings."

"Yes. It's only natural," Revna adds.

My mother passes a tissue to me, and I dab my face.

"Okay. Well. This is the nursery all prepped by the Daddies," I say with a smile. "They cleared the furniture, swapped the light fixtures, and painted in the wee hours of this morning."

Everyone praises their thoughtfulness as I grin happily.

We spend the next couple of hours on the nursery's layout and drafting lists for purchases. By the time we finish, we set the whole pup plan.

Wren moves to the sofa next to me and taps her tablet, waking the screen from an adorable photo of her and Tag's triplets.

"So, before you get too far in your pregnancy and forget your own name, launch Signy's Secret Cache. I'll help you," she says. Her mink brown eyes glow with the excitement of a new project.

I consider for a moment, wondering if it would be too much at once. However, my goal of opening my luxury online boutique brought me to New York. Without it, who knows when I would have met Garrett, Dolph, and Colin? It's as fated as we are.

"Excellent idea, Wren! Let's do it."

Sage joins us.

"Remember, I offered to help too, since I started my line of luxury custom-made jewelry."

Sage's Gems & Jewels is the hottest jewelry store in

Miami. All the socialites line up to request pieces from her collections. Waiting lists are the norm. Fortunately, I have the family inside track with first dibs. If Signy's Secret Cache can be half as successful, I'll achieve my goal.

"Yes, thanks so much! We need inventory, models, and photographers. I narrowed down the fulfillment companies. They're waiting for my decision—"

"Well, sweetheart, the moms will leave you to your business plans. We're going into the city for pup shopping," my mother says.

"Thank you! I can't wait to see what you come back with," I say, rising and hugging each of them. We chat as I walk them to the front door.

When I return to the family room, Maya grins at me.

"You had me at model. I'm more than happy to pose for you," she says.

And with her banging body, Maya can wear anything and make it look fantastic.

"And me at inventory," Vera adds. "I love shopping, and there's no place like New York City to do it. Look at all we bought during your bachelorette day. Imagine how well we can stock an online boutique!"

We laugh as she spreads her arms wide.

"Then let's get down to business. Shall we?" Wren asks.

"Indeed, we shall," I respond. "Let's convene our meeting in my office. With some fresh cookies and tea."

"Oh, and did we mention the cravings?" Sasha asks with a grin.

We laugh as we head through the mansion to the wing with my office.

Later that night, Garrett, Dolph, Colin, and I cuddle up on the semi-circular sofas around the firepit on the flagstone patio. I surprised them with fixings for yummy s'mores while I share the day's events.

"I love that you made the nursery into a blank canvas. Wren promised to paint a mural. She did an amazing one for the triplets. I can't wait to see what she comes up with for our nursery."

"That's very nice of her. Tell us what she needs. We'll have it ready when she returns to paint," Garrett says as he feeds a s'more to me.

I moan as the warm milk chocolate melts on my tongue. Smacking my lips, I ask for more. He grins and lifts the morsel to my mouth, then dabs the corner where the marshmallow stuck.

Colin leans over and licks the spot and hums in the back of his throat.

"The best s'more I've ever eaten," he says, brushing his lips over mine. "I wonder what else tastes better on Signy?"

Dolph chuckles wickedly and scoops a handful of marshmallows from the bag. He holds one between his fingers and cocks an eyebrow.

"I wonder how many of these we can fit into Signy's pussy before we have to eat them out?"

My mouth drops.

Holy shit!

The world tilts as Garrett flips me to my back. He lifts

my maxi dress around my waist, then drapes one leg over the back of the sofa and rests my head in his lap. Colin holds my other leg as he kneels beside me. Dolph settles on his belly.

"Let's get you wet to slide the marshmallows in easily. The more for us to eat."

He swipes his tongue from my puckered hole, along my pussy lips, to my throbbing clit.

My eyes close on a drawn-out moan.

He feasts on my pussy until my juices slide down the curve of my ass to puddle beneath my hips. I whimper when his tongue disappears, only to be replaced by his fingers as he pushes a marshmallow deep inside of me. One by one, he fills my pussy.

The odd sensation adds to my arousal. It builds as his fingers avoid my engorged clit. My hips circle to chase his touch for the place I need it most. My moan turns into a yelp when the tips of his fingers spank my pussy.

"Keep still, Naughty Girl."

Garrett glides his hands along my flanks, then presses his palms into my hip bones to hold me in place. I mewl and beg for relief.

Instead, Colin drips warm, melted milk chocolate on my tits, swirling extra around my peaked nipples. They stiffen further as my back bows. Which brings my mouth close to the waistband of Garrett's joggers, where the tip of his dick peeks out.

My tongue darts from my mouth to lap the pearl of pre-cum, then twirls around the plum-shaped head. As he groans, I moan. A glance down my body reveals Dolph's mouth enveloping my pussy while his tongue prods at a marshmallow buried inside.

"Mouth back here, Little Wolf," Garrett growls as he removes one hand from my hips and yanks his joggers past his ass. "Suck me and make me cum down your throat."

My pussy clenches at his command. A mewl slips from my mouth as it closes around his tip again.

"You will not leave me out, Little Wolf," Colin growls.

He grasps my hand and wraps it around his turgid length, already throbbing with need. Knowing he thrives on erotic pain, I squeeze and tug on his cock. He rewards me with a full-belly groan as his head falls back, eyes closed.

Dolph's lips brush against my sensitive clit. My hips buck, only for Garrett to press me back into the sofa. His cock slips from my mouth. He taps the shaft against my lips, demanding re-entry. I oblige and open wide. He slides it along my flattened tongue until it glides down my throat. It relaxes to give him access. He groans. I gag.

"Such a good girl."

"You mean such a *tasty* girl," Dolph corrects as he sits back on his haunches and chews a pussy-juice-soaked marshmallow. "De-fucking-licious."

I moan around Garrett's cock at their praise. The vibration triggers his release. His hands hold my jaw as he fucks my mouth.

"Damn... Look how your dick stretches her neck,"

Colin groans as his hips snap in time with Garrett's thrusts. *"Fuuuck.* I'm about to blow…"

Both detonate with roars.

"Swallow it all. Every. Drop."

My pussy leaks with more arousal, soaking the marshmallows still inside. Dolph groans and lowers his mouth for more. His tongue lashes my clit, then wraps around it to suck and teeth nip.

As I keen, Garrett's cock slips from my mouth. He grunts in satisfaction. I cum hard.

Drifting off, a smile spreads across my face.

One thing's for sure, being pregnant won't stop my mates from wanting me or me from wanting them.

arrett

"Are you sure you're feeling all right, Signy?"

"You've been pushing yourself these last few months."

"You can join the launch party via video conference."

Signy narrows her eyes, pops a hip, and folds her arms over her tits—doubled in size over the last eight months.

Although the most delectable, those aren't the only changes. My mouth waters at the extra plump nipples. Her tits overflow my hands now. When she rides me reverse cowgirl, they bounce from my hands and catch her chin. When I told her she was going to give herself a black eye if her tits keep growing, she punched my arm and burst into tears. Boy, did Dolph and Colin ream me out for that joke. I apologized nonstop until she threatened to never speak to me again if I didn't stop it already.

Since she's carrying fraternal twins, her belly expanded to accommodate their growth. I love to spoon her and cradle her belly. Dolph massages oils into her tits and belly every night to keep her skin supple. Colin sits her on his lap and places his ear on her belly to listen for our pups' movements. When she first complained about gaining weight, we told her we love her new curves as much as we do her pre-pregnancy figure. The beatific smile that bloomed on her face stole my breath away.

She refuses to cut her hair—something about stunting the pups' hair growth. As if a wolf shifter won't have hair. Still, we indulge her. We take turns shampooing and conditioning her hair as she lounges in the spa tub we installed for her in our en suite bathroom. I swear I've gained at least ten pounds of muscle on my right biceps from blow drying her hair that now tips the under curve of her voluptuous ass.

The added bulk proved useful since Dolph insisted we assemble the cribs, bassinets, and the changing tables. Who knew furniture for little beings could be so complicated and have thousands of parts? But the pride that spread in our chests when Signy cried tears of joy at the finished pieces made it all worth it.

The nursery is her masterpiece—a haven for our pups. She decorated it in earth and water tones of blue, green, brown, and cream with touches of yellow.

In the sitting room, a room-sized organic silk and wool rug rests atop the bleached hardwood floors. The open area proves perfect for the pups to crawl and learn to walk without falling onto the less-forgiving floor. To anchor the space, two sets of gliders flank the window seat, bassinets stand next to the wall opposite the fireplace. On each side of the double doors, toy chests stand with shelves above filled with stuffed animals. Naturally, three giant wolves with black, gold, and tawny fur stand guard on one side of the fireplace. To balance the other side, a smaller wolf with black fur and a white patch on the back stands facing the bedroom doors to watch over the pups within.

Signy kept the bedroom minimal. Two cribs, changing tables, and two gliders with another rug fill the space. The walk-in closets and dressing area hold neatly organized clothing and accessories. She fitted the en suite bathroom with pup-sized tubs and loads of organic linens.

Wren came through on her promise to paint a stunning mural. She brought the outside in with a recreation of the ocean view outside the windows. It's so realistic, the pups will recognize the panorama once they're older, especially the images of their fathers with their pregnant mother sitting on a picnic blanket in the foreground. Wren captured us perfectly, down to the detail of the pink and blue diamond pendant around Signy's neck.

It's the gift we gave to her after the ultrasound revealed a male pup and a female pup. A goofy grin still pops on my face when I think of the moment the examination room filled with the sound of two heartbeats. That is after

Natalie explained there was nothing wrong with the odd beats, rather Signy was carrying two pups.

Colin whooped, and fist pumped the air.

Dolph stood stunned.

My face split in a smile.

Signy burst into tears.

Between hiccups, she explained she had a dream of a male pup and a she-wolf pup playing in the surf. When she called to them, they waved and ran to hug her. She dropped to her knees in the sand and wrapped her arms around them as they giggled, kissing her face.

The abundance of love that came through our bond from her brought tears to our eyes. Even Natalie wiped her face and sniffled. She stepped from the exam room to give us a moment of privacy.

We gathered around Signy and placed our hands on her pups' bump while we rumbled deep in our chests to soothe her. We leaned together to absorb the poignant moment and imprint it on our minds forever.

That night, while Signy slept, I flew into the city for a private appointment at Harry Winston. The manager met me. I asked for a unique piece that symbolizes fraternal twins. He returned from the vault with the flawless ten-carat pink diamond and ten-carat blue diamond pendants on a platinum necklace. I FaceTimed Dolph and Colin. They agreed it's the quintessential symbol. When she woke the next morning, we gifted it to her and made love for hours.

She vowed to take the very best care of herself and rest when needed.

Well…

"We will go to your launch party"—she claps her hands, then stops when I raise mine—"However, we will not stay all night. Natalie cannot give an exact date since you carry twins. But we know you're due soon. So, rest. Remember, Little Wolf?"

Her cheeks pinken as her hands rest on her pups' bump. She nibbles the corner of her mouth, then nods.

"Fine. I promise to pay close attention to my body and how our pups feel," she says and looks at each of us.

"There's our good girl," Colin smirks.

"Now, can we go?"

"Yes," I say and extend my elbow to her.

She loops her arm through mine, and we leave our private suite at Club Sol & Mani New York—a former bank in Manhattan's Financial District, close to Moen, Inc.'s headquarters.

She and Wren decided it was the best venue for the party since Signy themed her first curated collection, *Love Signy*—her hormones told her to. It aligns perfectly with Valentine's Day. So, what better venue than a luxury BDSM sex club?

We closed it for her private event but included the club's VIPs on the invite list. She expects wolf shifters from around the globe to attend. For her human clientele, she's hosting social media live events in a week to give the wolf shifters first claim on pieces—no pun. They'll have access to exclusive clothing and lingerie designers created for her boutique.

The collection is impressive. But the gown she wears tops all.

Signy epitomizes sexy in a hot red number. It's a play on Shibari with a rope of shimmering red lamé over one shoulder bound to the opposite side of the strapless neckline. The rope zags between her tits to loop behind her back, around the opposite hip, and to gather beneath her pups' bump. The rope draws up the fabric, parting to a full-leg slit. Her long, lithe leg slips out as though playing peek-a-boo between the sheets. The hem cascades like the sheets fell to the floor during wild fucking.

And that's what we wanted to do. Rip the gown off, tie her to the St. Andrew's Cross, and make her cum all over our dicks. Except she growled at us. Actually growled and bared her elongated fangs. Even Colin gaped, shocked speechless.

Dolph—ever the comfort giver—saved us from being gutted by opening the flat blue suede case and telling her Happy Valentine's Day. Her scowl changed to a smile at the ruby and diamond earrings, necklace, bracelet, and ring nestled on a blue suede pillow. I took advantage of her distraction and clasped the necklace on her, followed by the other pieces. She thanked us with tears in her eyes as she clipped the earrings on. Crisis averted. We gathered around her and held her close.

With Signy on my arm, we enter Exhibition. Now,

decorated for the event with models on platforms and guests fully clothed in black-tie and gowns milling about, sipping signature Champagne cocktails.

Normally, the club's sections focus on the distinct elements of the lifestyle. Exhibition where demonstrations and performance rooms provide entertainment—or inspiration. The Dungeon a spacious section devoted to public forms of BDSM play. Those not in the lifestyle may think it's a medieval dungeon for torture with the St. Andrew's Crosses, spanking benches, chains suspended from the ceiling, and more. To us, the pieces and assorted whips, floggers, canes, and implements are only to be expected. And enjoyed by all partners. For those who prefer privacy, they may reserve suites—each outfitted for its theme. We maintain our private suite for our use only.

"Signy!"

Wren waves as she teeters towards us on sky-high strappy sandals.

Signy attempted the same. But we nixed that idea. No way will she strut about on five inches at eight-months pregnant with twins. Nope. She switched to a three-inch pair of glittery slingbacks. Her slight pout proved she agreed with us but didn't want to admit it.

Still, I hold her elbow as she slips from my side to greet Wren.

"This looks amazing! Thank you!" Signy gushes, embracing the petite brunette.

"Hey," Tag says in his usual grumpy way. Although since mating sunshiney Wren, he's less prickly.

As the four of us shake his hand, her brothers and their mates, along with Randel and Vera, join us. Soon guests gather around asking Signy about the collection. Dolph, Colin, and I stay next to her, not willing to let her out of our sight.

"It's time for your speech before the fashion show," Wren says an hour later. "Come, let's get you to the stage."

She grins up at us as she loops arms with Signy.

"I've got her. But you can stay close," she smirks.

I glance at Tag. He shrugs, used to Wren being busy.

As instructed, the three of us follow and stand at the edge of the stage. The lights dim, and a hush falls over the crowd. The spotlights focus on Signy.

She's radiant. The lights pick up the shimmering reds of her gown and dazzle on her jewelry. But it's the glow in her ice blue eyes that outshines all.

"Good evening, friends. Thank you for celebrating the launch of Signy's Secret Cache with me tonight. As some of you know, I love fashion and making females look elegant and sexy!"

She pauses as knowing laughter fills the space.

"A genuine clothes wolf!"

She laughs as Viggo teases.

"Absolutely! Thank you, brother. It's been my goal to create an online luxury boutique curated with pieces I collect from designers I adore and from up-and-coming designers. Like the one who dressed me tonight. I think she did an excellent job of accentuating the curves of my pregnant body, including my pups' bump!"

This time, applause and wolf whistles resound.

A male shifter who's a bit too enthusiastic flinches and backs away as I snarl in his face.

"Now, for the fashion show!" Signy ends her speech with a broad smile.

Dolph leaps onto the stage to help her down the steps while Colin and I reach out for her hands. Safely back with us, Dolph tucks her into his side while we flank them. He heads for the throne Wren situated on one side of the runway. Signy smiles and nods at the guests seated on other chairs, then sits. We take the chairs reserved for us.

Maya opens and closes the show with a sexy strut. Viggo stands each time, letting all present know she's his mate.

The show ends with the models walking out to clap before Signy. She stands and blows kisses at them while the guests applaud and shout *bravo*. Her excitement travels across our bond. We kiss her face and clap, proud of her achievement after so many obstacles and life changes.

"What a success, babe," I murmur in her ear, over the cheers. "Congratulations!"

"Thank you, my lo—"

She gasps and glances down.

Liquid splashes on my shoes.

I frown.

"Babe?"

"What the..."

"Did you pee yourself? I warned you not to drink that

glass of water before we left. You know your bladder can't handle it now."

Signy clutches her pups' bump with one hand and grips my forearm with the other. Her awe-stricken eyes lift to mine. Face flushed crimson.

"M—My water broke."

igny

"Not a chance, Signy."

"Those shoes are too high."

"You can wear them tonight with your legs wrapped around my neck."

Before I can protest, the dull ache in my lower back increases. My lips purse as I gauge the level of pain. Natalie described the symptoms of pre-labor as cramps, aches, and pressure. I've had the dull ache for a few hours. But she says it can last up to twelve hours for my cervix to dilate fully. I have plenty of time to go to the launch. But I won't wear these sky-high strappy sandals.

I put them back in their shoe bags and select a pair of red crystal-embellished slingbacks. Thankfully, I thought to buy an alternate style. Dolph helps me slip them on. I groan blissfully as he massages my calves.

"When we return to the suite, I'll give you a full-body massage with your favorite oils. How's that sound?" he asks and stands, helping me to my feet.

I lean against his chest and sigh contentedly.

"Divine, my love. Thank you."

When we walk out of the closet, Garrett and Colin raise their eyebrows, then lower their eyes, caressing my body. If I weren't so achy, my pussy would soften to prepare for a sound fucking. But not at all. Instead, I growl and flash my fangs. I'm as shocked as they are at my extreme reaction.

The incredible ruby and diamond jewelry suite Dolph presents flips my raging hormones switch off. Tears and thank you replace muttered curses. *Gah!*

As we leave our suite and walk the long way to Exhibition, I offer a prayer of thanks for the three-inch heels and Garrett's arm to hold. The dull ache and the snappish behavior fade as we enter the space with the models and guests. My dream come true plays out before me.

I gaze in wonder at the fabulous job Wren did to create a sumptuous boudoir. Soft, sensual music plays from a hidden surround-sound system. Sultry scents of jasmine, ylang-ylang, and rose suffuse the space. Dozens of antique French armoires display blouses, dresses, and lingerie from their open doors and drawers. Artfully arranged silk scarves, belts, gloves, and hats drape over antique dressing tables. Clusters of velvet-upholstered chaise lounges and oversized suede poufs atop Aubusson rugs provide seating areas for the guests.

They lounge or move about looking at pieces from the premier collection, *Love Signy*. With my enhanced hearing, I pick up bits of their conversations. All positive, thank the gods. My heart soars with excitement.

"Signy!"

My smile widens as Wren bustles over.

"This looks amazing! Thank you!"

As we exclaim over the success so far, our family and more guests join us. I beam with their words of congratulations. When Wren announces it's time for my speech and the fashion show, butterflies flutter in my belly. But as we step forward, I realize it's more than butterflies. I bite my lip to hold in a groan.

"Are you all right?" Wren asks, staring up at me, her eyebrow arched as she studies my face.

I nod and brave a smile, not wanting the night to end before I welcome the guests. Gods willing, I last until after the fashion show. I rub my pups' bump and ask them to give me half an hour, then take a cleansing breath.

The gods grant my wish. But not a second more.

"What a success, babe. Congratulations!" Garretts murmurs.

"Thank you, my lo—"

A cramp grips my belly. I gasp in pain. Liquid gushes to the floor. I glance down.

"Babe?"

"What the..."

"Did you pee yourself? I warned you not to drink that glass of water before we left. You know your bladder can't handle it now."

My hand clutches the underside of my pups' bump while the other hand grabs Garrett's arm. The sleeve of his bespoke tuxedo crumples under my grip. I pant through the pain of another cramp and stare up at him.

"M—My water broke."

His eyes bug as his jaw hits the floor, like a cartoon character. If the pain wasn't so intense, I'd laugh out loud at his comical expression.

"Wait. What?" Dolph asks.

I stagger, clutching Garrett tighter.

"Fuck that," Colin says and scoops me in his arms. "Out of the way! Move!"

He barrels through the surprised guests. Burying my face in Colin's neck, I wrap an arm around his shoulder and the other cradles my belly.

Garrett and Dolph charge ahead of us, clearing the way.

"How far are your contractions, Signy?"

I peek over at Natalie.

"A few minutes?"

I grunt as another hits me. I swear it was a foot. *Don't beat your Mommy. Not nice.*

"Okay, breath like I taught you," Natalie says, then speaks to Colin. "We have time to get her back to the island. Is the helicopter at Moen, Inc. like I asked?"

"Yes," they answer in unison.

Not bothering with the SUV in traffic, Colin runs me

through the streets. I keep my eyes closed and breathe while speaking to our pups. Rather begging them to wait until we get to the pack hospital.

"The other helicopters are at the heliport. We'll meet you at the hospital," Jagger says. "We love you, little sis. You and the pups will be fine."

He's gone before I can respond.

The ride up to Moen, Inc.'s roof is quick since we used their high-speed private elevator. We climb aboard with Natalie and Doc. They make me comfortable with towels on the plush leather seat and a cashmere throw on my lap. As I gasp with another contraction, Garrett dabs my face with a cool cloth while Dolph removes my slingbacks and Colin rubs my hand. Their rumbling helps. A bit.

The pilot sets the helicopter on the lawn in front of the hospital. Nurses rush forward with a gurney. They transfer me and race inside to my room. I watch as they cut my gown off and discard it. A pang of sadness hits me. Then I roll my eyes. Get a grip Signy…

Dressed in a hospital gown, Natalie returns to exam me.

"You're almost there, Sig. It won't be long before you hold your pups in your arms."

I return her smile with a grimace as another contraction rocks me.

She checks again and shakes her head.

"Correction. Get ready to push."

"Already?"

"Are you sure?"

"Oh, damn."

Natalie chuckles.

"You guys get ready, too. She'll need you."

They shed their bow ties and jackets, then toss their cufflinks on the table and roll up their sleeves. Each takes a position beside me on the bed. Garrett and Colin take a hand while Dolph strokes my hair.

"You've got this, Little Wolf."

"We love you so much."

"You're so brave, baby girl."

I smile as best I can.

"Love you too."

Three hours later, I hold Amora and Arkyn to my breasts. White cotton blankets cover them to their necks. Amora's ebony hair and Arkyn's blond hair poke out. Pairs of blue and golden eyes peer up at me. Amora resembles Garret and me while Arkyn is a miniature Dolph and Colin. The perfect combination of the four of us in our pups.

We gave them names with special meanings. Garrett wanted Amora for little eagle since his father Arne's name means eagle. We agreed since Amora also means love. Arkyn is perfect for the male from a long line of pack Alphas since it means eternal king's son. Dolph and Colin left the names to us. They're ecstatic one pup takes after them.

Two days later, we go home and settle Amora and Arkyn in their beautiful nursery. Our families visit and take turns holding them. Garrett, Dolph, and Colin hover, not wanting their pups far from them. I sit back and smile, thrilled we finally made it to our happily ever after.

Once we tuck the pups in their cribs, we sit cuddled under cashmere blankets before the fireplace in our suite's sitting room. The gold and red flames flicker as the scent of pine fills the air. I sigh and snuggle against Garrett's chest with Colin behind me and Dolph massaging my legs.

"Happy, Little Wolf?" He asks.

"Beyond happy, my loves."

"So are we, babe," Colin says.

Garrett rumbles in his chest.

"You are ours, Signy. Forever ours."

EPILOGUE

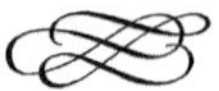

5 Years Later
Garrett

"I DON'T KNOW about you. But I think Signy's been acting strange lately."

"Yeah. She practically snapped my head off when I asked her to pass a fork to me. And she was in the kitchen, standing next to the utensils draw getting her own fork."

I nod, recalling how she swatted me out of the shower this morning, accusing me of invading her space.

"We're landing in five minutes, Alpha," the helicopter pilot says.

So caught up in thoughts of Snappy Signy, I didn't notice how close we are to Moen, Inc. A glance out the window shows the Manhattan skyline bathed in the pink and blue rays of dawn breaking. I collect my mobile from the table and check my calendar for the day's schedule.

Meetings with suppliers, a lunch, and the afternoon executive team meeting fill my day.

The helicopter lands, and we disembark. As we take the stairs from the roof to the top floor, my mobile dings with a text. Thyra's name appears on the screen. It's been a while since we spoke. I read her message and smirk. Yeah, right.

"What's that snort for?"

I shake my head at Colin.

"You know Thyra."

"Been a minute, huh?"

"I'd say," Dolph responds.

I type a response and slip the mobile in my suit jacket pocket, then stride for my office suite. Time for work.

Throughout the day, I send text messages to Signy since she doesn't respond to me through our bond. Her brief responses further prove something is up with our mate. I make it my mission to find out when we return to the island.

DOLPH

"HEY, babe. Checking to see how your day is going. Call back when you get a chance. Love you."

I toss the mobile on my desk and spin the chair to face the wall of floor-to-ceiling windows. FiDi's backdrop of glittering skyscrapers, Wall Street, and banks dissolves as I consider what's going on with Signy.

Our lives have been pretty great these past five years. Amora and Arkyn celebrated their fifth birthday in Miami with their cousins. They're less dependent on her since they're older and advanced for their age. Which leaves her more time for Signy's Secret Cache. Her boutique thrives with waitlists for most of the collections. Then there's our sex life. It's as scorching as ever, with frequent stays at Club Sol & Mani New York. So, I'm perplexed by Signy's irritable behavior.

"Dolph, your two o'clock arrived."

My administrative assistant's announcement over the intercom brings my mind back to the office and the rest of my workday.

"Send them in, thank you."

I rise and slip my suit jacket on over my vest and adjust my dress shirt sleeves. My next meeting. The distraction I need until we get home and find out what the hell's going on with our mate.

～

COLIN

. . .

"The quarterly analysis shows an increase in demand for…"

Ordinarily, I pay close attention during the executive team meeting. As Chief Legal Counsel, I need to be aware of any potential for a lawsuit or for violations of contracts with our partners. But today?

Damn.

Signy preoccupies my mind.

She nearly stabbed me with the fork when she handed it to me. I thought she'd be excited since I brought home dinner—her favorite dish, the cheesy potato gratin from Le Gratin. It's been a couple of weeks since we ate at the restaurant.

Maybe that's what's wrong. She wants more date nights.

Hell, if that'll stop her bite, we'll take her out every damn night.

I grip the back of my neck and stretch it from side to side. Focus, Voll.

"We have word of new technology for—"

Oh, gods…

My head snaps up as my cock punches the zipper of my suit trousers. Pupils dilate. A growl slips from my mouth.

The presenter backs away as the rest of the staff glances around nervously.

Garrett, Dolph, Colin… I need you. Now! I'm at the cabin.

I jump to my feet at the same time as Garrett and Dolph, then scramble across the table directly to the conference room doors. Papers, pens, and cups scatter. We burst through the doors into the corridor, ripping the ties from our necks. Our long strides get us to the rooftop stairs in seconds.

"We need the helicopter for the island. Now!" Garrett snarls into his mobile.

Oooo, hurry... Please...

We're on our way, Little Wolf.

Don't you dare touch yourself before we get there!

And we'll know if you do, Naughty Wolf.

We bound up the stairs and rush through the door. Our feet pound the roof as we pace, waiting for the pilot. He and the flight attendant emerge minutes later.

"Hurry up!" Garrett commands as he jerks the door open and jumps inside.

We follow, chests heaving.

The crew races across the roof and hops in. The pilot lifts off after the system check and communication with the air traffic controller. We whiz through the air.

"Set us down at the cabin in the woods," Garrett says as we near Moen Island.

Is that your helicopter I hear?

Yes!

Thank the gods... Ooooh...

While the landing gear hovers above the ground, I slide the door back.

"As Arkyn and Amora say, 'last one there is a rotten egg!'" I shout and jump from the helicopter.

The wind whips Garrett and Dolph's curses away as I

race across the snow-covered field, stripping as I go, then bound through the door.

"Signy!" I bellow as the honey sweet aroma of her heat fills my nostrils. I throw my head back and howl.

"Fuuuck!"

"She's in heat!"

I ignore Garrett and Dolph and follow her mouth-watering aroma to the bedroom. My hard cock leaks with pre-cum. I fist the thick shaft, readying it to pound into her fertile pussy and flood her womb with my seed. I stalk towards her, writhing in the middle of her nest.

Signy's feverish eyes lock on my cock. With a throaty moan, she falls back and spreads her legs, showing us her slick covered swollen pussy. A desperate groan falls from her mouth as her fingertips spread the delectable slick on her trembling thighs.

"Oh, yes, Little Wolf. Your fated mates will breed you once again."

THANK you for reading *Signy Forever* the happily ever after for Signy, Garrett, Dolph, and Colin! Their spicy romance is a standalone trilogy in the sizzling Billionaire Wolves Series of interconnecting stories featuring wolf shifter fated mates. Get a glimpse of their dynamism in other books.

Don't want it to be over? Need more?
Join my newsletter for an exclusive bonus epilogue with a
new pup for this foursome!
https://BookHip.com/MBTPQMD

IF YOU ENJOYED THIS BOOK, I would so appreciate your review as they make a huge difference for indie authors. Turn the page for a preview of the start to the Billionaire Wolves Series—*Jagger The Temptation: A Wolf Shifter Fated Mates Paranormal Romance.*

PREVIEW JAGGER THE TEMPTATION: A WOLF SHIFTER FATED MATES PARANORMAL ROMANCE

*J*agger

"THE QUARTERLY NUMBERS show an increase in profits. More than projected because of the opening of the beach-front resort in Charleston earlier than planned. The general manager reports the property sold out for the first four months…"

I nod as my Vice President of Hotels and Resorts for Larson Enterprises, Inc. continues his update. My mind focuses partially on his presentation.

For the last few weeks, I can't seem to focus. I don't know whether lack of sleep causes the lapse or something else. Dreams of another dominate my nights. They remain just out of reach, on the fringes. But it's their silent pleas for help that keep me tossing. A vibration from them of fear and sadness draws me closer. My instinct kicks in, and I want to save them, protect them.

Each dream brings me closer to them. But they remain just out of reach. I wake tangled in silk sheets. An arm extended as my hand reaches for them. Last night I called a name. However, as the last vestiges of the dream slipped away, the name dissolved with it.

I growl low in my chest in frustration.

My COO shifts his gaze to me. His wolf senses picked up my displeasure with ease.

I shake my head at Tag Dahl.

He cocks his head at me.

As my best friend, he's known me since we were pups. Born within a few weeks of each other—him to our pack's enforcer and me to our Alpha—Tag knows me as well as I know myself. I haven't mentioned my dreams to him, not that he'd think me nuts. No. I just don't know what they mean and if they warrant a conversation for analysis.

And Tag would delve into their meaning.

As my beta, he's my right-hand man. Anything that involves me and can impact our pack, he wants to solve the puzzle.

But this one will remain under wraps until I figure it out. So, I shake my head again and turn my attention back to the presentation. Even as I will my mind to pay full attention. I remove my personal hat. Then I firmly affix the one for my roles as CEO and Chairman of the Board of the luxury hotels, fine dining, clubs, and lounges company my family founded in Miami.

An hour later, a persistent Tag strides along with me to my suite of offices in The Larson Tower on Biscayne Bay. We pass through the executive floor as staff—wolf shifter and human—acknowledge us. The unaware humans often stare in awe at our formidable sizes. We're both six feet, seven inches of pure muscle and move with predatory grace. We nod in return but continue without pause.

I know Tag wants to find out what's up with me. I'll allow his henpecking since we're so close. Otherwise, I do not tolerate others in my business. No. One.

"Alpha, you have a few voicemails, sir."

"Thanks, Ginny," I respond to my administrative assistant as I open the double doors of my office. "Kindly hold my calls."

"What's up, Jagger?"

I bite back an irritated growl—lack of sleep will have you pissed, even at your best friend who only wants to help.

"You want a drink?" I ask as I unbutton the jacket of my bespoke three-piece Brioni suit and stride to the bar cart. It's after five-thirty, and I can use a stiff one before I head out to Club Sol & Mani for some much-needed sexual relief.

"Sure, thanks."

I take my time pouring two fingers of scotch into the Baccarat crystal tumblers. Absolutely no rush to have Tag pick at my psyche. My ears pick up his almost silent huff, and I chuckle to myself.

"Don't delay this conversation, Jag. You've been off for a few weeks now, and I've given you space," he says, then nods his thanks for the liquor. "What's up with you?"

Again, I allow him to question me, even though I'm his Alpha and my word is final.

I lower myself onto the dove gray tufted leather sofa in the seating area. Tag takes a chair opposite and places an ankle over a knee. I sip my drink as I consider my words. He knows better than to interrupt at this point.

"Dreams."

He cocks his head at the simple one-worded response. I shrug and take another sip.

"For the past few weeks, dreams invade my sleep. Every. Single. Night. Someone's in trouble. But I can't catch their name or where they are to help them," I sigh and stare out the window.

The panoramic view across Biscayne Bay with jet skiers and megayachts on its dazzling surface out to the azure Atlantic Ocean helps to quiet the inner turmoil my wolf and I sense. He turns his massive silvery white head to stare at me with accusatory ice blue eyes. It's as though he knows something I don't and pissed I'm not aware. I run my fingers through my white blond hair as I think on it, then shake my head. No clue.

"What do you recall?" Tag asks as he leans forward and places his elbows on his knees, the scotch tumbler balanced between his sizable hands.

I shrug.

"A brightness in the background prevents a clear view. I know it's outdoors since I hear the hum of insects and feel the warm sun on my skin. Naked skin. So, I must have shifted and returned to my human form."

Another sip of scotch, and I stand to pace my office.

Instinct tells me these are no ordinary dreams. But each morning I account for the whereabouts of my pack, and no one turns up missing. Not knowing who calls for my help drives me and my wolf mad.

I growl and toss back the rest of my scotch. A few long strides and I refill the tumbler.

"No one in our pack seems in trouble. I'll stop by the she-wolves' residences on my way home just to make sure. A few of our unmated males flew to New Orleans for the weekend. I'll shoot a text to them and make sure they didn't get into anything on Bourbon Street."

With a nod of agreement, I hold the decanter up. Tag declines a refill—ever the responsible one. Fine. It's not like wolf shifters can get drunk. Well, not too much. Our systems process substances differently from humans. All the better for us, especially when I'm in this pissy mood.

"Well, you know they say fated mates can have dreams about the other. The more frequent and intense they become, the closer the pair gets to their first encounter," Tag says. His emerald green eyes scan my face for a reaction. He knows I've waited all these years for my fated mate—and will continue to do so.

Despite my father's damn near daily persistence, I issue

the claiming bite and complete the mating bond with a single she-wolf. The last eleven years of nearly nonstop mating runs, with the she-wolves in my pack and those from nearby cities—hell, even overseas. Or galas at our hotels and mixers at our clubs, an accidental encounter, all to persuade me to select a she-wolf as my mate. None of them tempt me in the slightest.

All the she-wolves desire to bond with me. Then the supposed prince—and they were eager to lose their slippers and thongs for me to pick up——now the Alpha of the Miami Wolves Pack. Correction, *Billionaire Wolves of Miami* as the other packs refer to us. With good reason, since we're the most powerful pack in the South.

Several millennia ago, Scandinavian Viking wolf shifters sailed from the Old World and landed along the East Coast of what's now the United States. The six packs headed by best friends who sought new lands moved throughout the continent to form territories with ours settling here. We maintain close ties with our brethren through friendship, mating, and business. Plus, our Ruling Council gatherings keep us informed of happenings throughout the packs.

And even going that far and wide, I have yet to meet my fated mate. However, I will wait for her.

Hell, my wolf demands it as he gets agitated when he senses a she-wolf's burgeoning interest. Sure, he'll sit back while I fuck since it fills a need and doesn't equate to being mated. Wolf shifters—male and female—have strong sexual appetites. We don't have the same hang-ups as humans over casual sex, no sex before marriage, and whatever other bullshit they come up with. It's a part of our lives, just like eating or breathing. A need we won't suppress. Particularly with the built-up tension raging through my body. However, his pacing and snarls have increased recently, too.

So maybe Tag is on to something.

My *fated* mate.

A she-wolf whose scent I was born with teasing my nostrils. When she appears, I will recognize her by her distinct scent. No other will bear her uniqueness. Someday we will meet. I will give her my claiming bite, and we will have our mate bonding ceremony for all the clans to witness. I will make her mine forever.

The thought she may be in trouble makes my blood boil and my wolf snap his teeth, ears flat to his head. Our protective instinct on high alert.

So, I won't give up on finding my fated mate—or on us. No matter how many times my father bugs me about the need to bond with another. I'm no longer the teen who had to obey.

I am Alpha now.

"We're here, Alpha."

I glance up from my mobile screen and out the tinted window.

So focused on business emails, I didn't notice my driver

pull my Black Badge Rolls-Royce Cullinan into the driveway for Club Sol & Mani Miami. The flagship of six exclusive, luxury, members only BDSM clubs Larson Enterprises owns sits on Ocean Drive directly across from the Atlantic Ocean in a South Beach historic, beachfront gated mansion.

"Great, thank you, Cole," I respond. "I'll take it from here and will text when I'm ready to go home."

"Yes, Alpha. I'll get the door for you."

I wave him off and reach for the handle, only for the club's valet to open the door. A nod to Cole and a thanks in the form of a hundred to the young wolf shifter, and I stride to the scrolled wrought-iron and glass doors of the Spanish-style mansion. Laughter from members as they frolic in the mosaic-tiled pool within the sun-filled courtyard floats in the balmy evening air.

"Good evening, Alpha," the doorman says with a respectful bow of his head. I shake his hand and palm off another hundred. He thanks me as I move on.

"Hello, Alpha!" The two she-wolf greeters chorus cheerfully as I walk through the opulent lobby to the elevators. Another two C-notes and I'm on the elevator headed to my personal suite.

Tonight, I'll play in privacy rather than amongst other members in Exhibition where demonstrations and performance rooms provide entertainment—or inspiration. Nor will the Dungeon do, despite my affinity for the spacious section devoted to public forms of BDSM play. Those not in the lifestyle may think it's a medieval dungeon for torture with the St. Andrew's Crosses, spanking benches, chains suspended from the ceiling, and more. To me, the pieces and assorted whips, floggers, canes, and implements are only to be expected.

The soft thrum of sensual music greets me as I step out of the elevator and into the hallway. The rhythm vibrates through my core as intended to amp arousal for what lies behind the closed doors of the eight private suites. Members can reserve them in advance should they prefer the same privacy I wish for tonight.

Each suite decorated by theme has various BDSM pieces, implements, and toys. A nice variety of options to choose from. However, my suite remains for my personal use only.

I press my palm against the plate by the door of the corner suite, and the locks disengage.

"Good evening, Alpha."

My head jerks up. What the fuck?! I allow no one in my space without my consent. My ice blue eyes adjust to the candlelit room. On my custom-built mahogany wood, king-size bed cornered by four thick carved posters and a brass lattice canopy with rings strategically attached sits a she-wolf from my pack. And not just any she-wolf. The sable-haired hellion.

"Melissa, what the fuck are you doing in my suite?!" I snarl as I stalk towards her.

She jerks back as though slapped but recovers quickly. Fully naked, she rises from the bed with the prowess of a wolf in hunt mode and slinks towards me. Amber eyes glow in the candlelight. She tosses her waist-length sable brown hair over her shoulders. Her sleek figure with high perky tits tipped by puckered rosy nipples, flat belly, narrow waist, slim hips, and long, toned legs would make any male salivate.

Not me.

Even though I planned to fuck her tonight—after I *invited* her to my suite—my stomach churns at the thought as my wolf growls low in his broad chest. He's not happy, nor am I.

Melissa is one of my regular sexual partners. We scratch the itch for each other from time to time. However, it's not like we're exclusive. Many a she-wolf join me for carnal pleasures. As Melissa has with other males. And I've made it clear I am not interested in bonding with her.

But after this stunt, this may very well be the last time I hookup with her. If she thinks she can enter my domain uninvited, she's confused. And I will speak with the club manager about her gaining unapproved access.

I have no intention of giving Melissa any ideas.

Not happening.

For one, Melissa thinks she's the alpha since the other male wolf shifters in our pack bow down to her beauty and succumb to her whims. I won't have it.

Not to mention she's a bully. Another trait I will not tolerate. I treat everyone in our pack with respect. They may not be my equal, but I don't make them feel less than.

And the most important reason... She's not my fated

mate. The only wolf shifter who will enter my domain as she pleases.

My wolf agrees with a flick of his feathery tail.

"Melissa, I have told you we fuck. Nothing more"—I raise my hand to stop her response—"You have no right to enter my personal suite without my permission. None. Get dressed. I will inform the club manager not to allow you entry ever again. This is it. Do you understand?"

She blinks, then her mouth opens.

I fold my arms over my chest and stand with feet spread far apart in a dominant manner as I pin her with an arctic gaze.

Naturally, Melissa glares back and mimics my stance as her eyes blaze golden fire.

"Jag—"

"Alpha! Alpha, Melissa. And do not forget it. We may have fucked. But you will respect me as your Alpha. Get. Dressed. And. Go. Now."

She lifts her chin in defiance, then reconsiders when I slap my sizable palm on my muscular thigh. Her eyes widen at the warning. Then she scurries to the chair and gathers her clothes to her flushed chest.

"Yes, Alpha!" She exclaims.

With a stern eye, I watch as she dresses quickly.

Melissa stops at the door and glances at me over her shoulder. Her oval-shaped face pinched with worry. She knows she took it too far this time.

"Sorry, Alpha," she whispers, then opens the door and leaves.

I sigh and sink onto the bed.

Well, there goes the idea of releasing tension. More just built up.

With his tongue hanging out from the side of his mouth, my wolf yips. Ice blue eyes gleam with mirth. It's as though he laughs at my misfortune.

I growl at him and slump back on the navy blue silk pillows. My thoughts drift to my conversation with Tag. Perhaps fate doesn't want me with another since my mate will appear soon. My eyes close on a sigh.

Where are you?

~

Click the Image Below or Visit books2read.com/u/ mZEL2e For Your Copy

Jagger The Temptation: A Wolf Shifter Fated Mates
Paranormal Romance

WANT FREE BOOKS?

Want to know what happened to Jagger's best friend Dylan? Find out in *Dylan The Rogue: A Wolf Shifter Fated Mates Paranormal Romance* your FREE Book!

Click Cover Below or visit **bit.ly/ CLBooksDylanTheRogue** to subscribe to my newsletter for latest news and launches, books from my author friends, and sizzling reads in book promotions. Plus, start reading the steamy fated mates romance for bad boy wolf shifter Dylan.

To read her current works, visit her Ream Stories account bit.ly/CharmaineLouiseBooksCoterie.

ABOUT CHARMAINE LOUISE SHELTON

Charmaine Louise Shelton loves a dominant Alpha hero—human, shifter, or vampire—as long as he's a billionaire and sexy as sin! Her romance novels take readers into the heroes' glitzy, glamorous, steamy worlds as they chase after independent women who unexpectedly capture their hearts. Want to experience some more? Download a free book at CharmaineLouiseBooks.com! To read her current works, visit her Ream Stories account bit.ly/Charmaine LouiseBooksCoterie.

Find her at:
CharmaineLouiseBooks.com

Follow her on social media on your favorite channels below and **download your Free Book** at CharmaineLouise Books.com.

Fulfill Your Desires.

BB bookbub.com/authors/charmaine-louise-shelton
tiktok.com/@charmainelouisebooks
youtube.com/@charmainelouisebooks
facebook.com/CharmaineLouiseBooks
instagram.com/charmainelouisebooks
g goodreads.com/charmainelouisebooks

STEELE INTERNATIONAL, INC.
A BILLIONAIRES ROMANCE SERIES

Discover My Desires Sebastian & Lola Prequel

(Available Exclusively to Subscribers)

Fulfill My Desires Sebastian & Lola Part I

Heighten My Desires Sebastian & Lola Part II

Ignite My Desires Roger & Leonie Part I

Stoke My Desires Roger & Leonie Part II

Justify My Desires Roger & Leonie Part III

Deepen My Desires Sebastian & Lola Part III

Capture My Desires Malcolm & Starr Part I

Embrace My Desires Malcolm & Starr Part II

Cherish My Desires Malcolm & Starr Part III

Gift My Desires Sebastian & Lola First Christmas

STEELE INTERNATIONAL, INC. - JACKSON CORPORATION

A BILLIONAIRES ROMANCE SERIES CROSSOVER

NEW YORK

<u>Signy's Mates</u>

<u>Signy Claimed</u>

<u>Signy Forever</u>

<u>Series Playlist</u>

Complete List bit.ly/CharmaineLouiseSheltonBooksList

<u>CharmaineLouiseBooks.com</u>

To read her current works, visit her Ream Stories account <u>bit.ly/CharmaineLouiseBooksCoterie</u>.

DEDICATION

To my awesome and dedicated beta readers and ARC Team, my amazing author friends, and this incredible community for their support.

And most of all to you, my loyal readers who love these couples as much as I do.

Thank you!

Fulfill Your Desires.

xoxo
Charmaine Louise Shelton